The Pony Whisperer

Stables S.O.S.

Collect all the Pony Whisperer books:

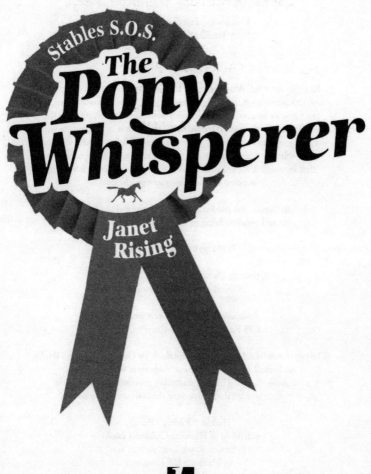

Stables S.O.S.

The Pony Whisperer

Janet Rising

h
Hodder
Children's
Books

A division of Hachette Children's Books

This edition first published in 2011
by Hodder Children's Books

I

ISBN 978 0 340 98846 6

Typeset in Garamond by Avon DataSet Ltd,
Bidford on Avon, Warwickshire

Printed and bound in Great Britain by
CPI Bookmarque Ltd, Croydon, Surrey

The paper and board used in this paperback by Hodder Children's Books
are natural recyclable products made from wood grown in
sustainable forests. The manufacturing processes conform to the
environmental regulations of the country of origin.

Hodder Children's Books
a division of Hachette Children's Books
338 Euston Road, London NW1 3BH
An Hachette UK Company
www.hachette.co.uk

To Di – happy horsey memories!

Chapter One

"So," said Drummer, fixing me with his deep brown eyes, "what's the plan? And don't tell me you *still* haven't got one."

I chewed the inside of my mouth and pulled a bit of a face. I was going to get nagged. Again. Because the fact was I hadn't got a plan. The promise I'd made at Christmas had progressed no further. *Yet*, I reminded myself.

"Haven't *you* got any ideas?" I asked him, attacking his tail with a plastic curry comb.

"Oi, what are you doing back there?" Drummer said, turning as far as his rope would allow to take a look. "You're not supposed to use one of those things on my tail, it pulls the hairs out."

"Your tail can stand a bit of thinning out," I told him, hacking away. My pony's black tail was more like

I

three tails, there was so much of it.

"Ouch!" bleated Drummer, theatrically.

No, I still didn't have a plan. You are useless, Pia, I silently scolded myself. No-one at Laurel Farm, where I keep Drummer, my bay, part-Arab pony, had come up with a plan, either. If we didn't get one in place soon, it would be too late.

"Bambi's getting panicky about it," Drummer told me, unnecessarily.

"I know, I know, I'm trying, we all are."

"Try harder!" Drum instructed me.

It's something, isn't it, getting told off by your own pony, even if it is understandable.

"There," I told him, "you're done. You can go back out in the field with the others."

"About time," Drummer grumbled.

Leading him across the yard to the field gate I gave him the carrot he knew was in my pocket; as I did, my fingers brushed against the tiny stone statue which is always there. Two crunches and the carrot was gone – and so was Drum, trotting across the grass to meet up with his mates, particularly Bambi.

Even though I'd brushed out his saddle mark after our early ride, and tidied up his mane and tail (or perhaps *because* of it!), Drummer went through the

2

same ritual of getting down to roll, and because today was the first warm, sunny day of spring, he left a carpet of his moulting winter hair behind on the dirt as he rose and shook himself, dust and more loose hairs gently falling around him in a cloud. I knew the birds would soon be swooping down to claim the discarded coat for their nests.

"Hey, Pia!" I heard someone shout and looking around I spotted Katy over the other side of the field, stretching herself up like a meerkat to look over the hill. I wondered where everyone had gone. Hooking Drum's headcollar over the gate I walked over to find Bean and James with Katy, sitting on the grass and enjoying the view.

"Hiya!" Bean greeted me as I flopped down beside them. They had picked a great spot – the ground fell away and we could see the countryside beyond the ponies' field below us.

"Have you been riding?" I asked.

"Nah!" sighed James, "it's too hot. Moth's taking ages to shed her winter coat now her clip has grown out so she'll only get all sweaty and lose weight."

"That's because you go everywhere at a hundred miles an hour," Katy remarked, disapprovingly.

"Moth hates hanging about," James replied, by

3

way of explanation.

"Do I spy some sweets?" I asked.

"Yeah, help yourself," said Bean, throwing me the bag, "before they're all gone!" she said, shooting James a meaningful look.

"What are you all doing out here?" I asked.

"Getting our heads around a plan," Bean said.

"I wish!" exclaimed James. "We're *trying* to think up a plan."

"No luck yet," Katy said. "It's all your fault, Pia, it was your idea."

"And now we're the ones doing all the work!" added James, swivelling around and winking at me.

My legs instantly jellified. I don't mean they actually turned to jelly, they just felt as though they had. James can do that to me. I wish he couldn't, it's most disconcerting and very inconvenient. I mean, what if there was a sudden emergency and I had to get up and go somewhere fast? I couldn't do that with jellified legs, could I?

We all lay looking at the view or the sky and as my legs gradually returned to their normal solid-feeling state I searched my mind once again for inspiration. A brilliant plan wasn't going to invent itself, I thought. We had to come up with one! And Katy was right, it

4

had been my idea. My mind stayed blank, just like it does when I try to make polite conversation with my dad's annoying girlfriend, Skinny Lynny, who he left me and Mum for.

I couldn't believe we still had no plan in place. Christmas was months behind us – but since then there had always been so much going on that putting aside any time for serious thinking had been out of the question. January had been bitterly cold and all the taps on the yard had frozen solid, making watering the ponies difficult. Poor Mrs Collins, who lived in her house on the yard at Laurel Farm, had fed a hose from her kitchen sink and we had all stood outside in a queue like wartime refugees with our ponies' buckets, which had taken ages to fill. And because the ground in the field had been so hard and rutted, the ponies had been in for most of the month as we'd been scared they'd damage their legs, so we'd had to exercise them in the outdoor school, all at the same time – which had been hairy. I'd lost count of the number of times I'd almost fallen – no, make that 'been bucked' – off. The ponies were so fresh it had taken all our concentration to stay on them and keep them moving.

Then February had brought deep snow – which had been even worse because I couldn't cycle to the yard, and my mum's car wasn't man enough to tackle the snow, so Dee-Dee's mum Sophie, in that can-do way of hers, had acted as a taxi service in her huge 4X4, ferrying everyone from their homes to the yard and back again (James said she only did it because she would have had to have mucked out and fed our ponies otherwise, but Katy told him he was looking a gift horse in the mouth). But at least we'd been able to turn the ponies out in the snow – they'd gone ballistic! It had been really funny watching them gallop about and roll in it. They'd all looked like they'd been sugar-frosted! We'd even managed to ride them on the bridle-paths in the snow at the weekend, which had been amazing – but not exactly good for thinking up plans because we'd either been concentrating on where we were going, or laughing so much.

March had been a month for catching up and struggling with the thaw, April had brought the Easter holidays and some events which we'd all entered and now, unbelievably, it was May. Already! Time to get cracking because the deadline was rushing towards us – it was now only two months away – and things were getting desperate!

I lay in the sunshine and racked my brains. At last we had time to think. But then, just as we found some time to give the problem our full attention, yet another diversion arrived. Only today, relaxing in the field, we didn't know just how big a diversion it was going to be.

"Uh-oh, look out, two more lost souls," remarked Katy, twirling a blade of grass around her mouth and squinting against the sunlight. Lazily, I turned and followed her gaze, frowning as my eyes found their target. It was a man and a woman, standing in the ponies' field, looking around and pointing.

"Go and tell them to clear off," murmured James, rudely. "Honestly, some hikers think they can just walk anywhere – including our ponies' field. And they're ruining my concentration," he added.

"They don't look much like hikers," mused Katy. "They're both wearing suits. Who hikes in a suit?"

"Who cares?" mumbled Bean. "Are there any more sweets, Pia?"

"Nope, all gone," I told her, putting the last one in my mouth and chewing. I refused to be distracted. How rubbish we were at inspiration, I thought, still planless. Total, complete, pants. Time was ticking away and we still had nothing. Nada. Zilch. Big, fat zero. Frankly, my head hurt.

"They *must* be hikers," sighed James, shielding his eyes against the sun as he looked across the field, "because they're looking at a map."

"They're freaking Tiffany out," Bean said huffily.

I looked over to where Tiffany had been grazing with Katy's blue roan gelding Bluey and James's chestnut mare Moth. Bean's palomino mare was doing her best giraffe impersonation, head high, eyes out on stalks, staring at the two strangers in dismay. You'd think they were a couple of yeti, not just an ordinary man and a woman. The trouble with Tiffany is that she's unnerved by anything out of the ordinary. And, it has to be said, quite a lot of things *in* the ordinary, too.

"Everything scares Tiffany," James snorted.

"She's really brave!" Bean protested, indignantly.

"*What?*" asked Katy, bewildered.

"Explain!" I demanded.

"OK, so she is scared of everything but she still goes past things for me, things your ponies aren't scared of," Bean said. "It's easy for your ponies, but Tiffany has to face her fears every day. That makes her *extra* brave."

"One-hundred-percent Bean logic," Katy sighed, lying back down in the grass and gazing up at the sky.

"I wonder how Dee's getting on," I said. She had gone to a show with her pony, Dolly Daydream.

I imagined them cantering around the ring looking fabulous, accepting a red rosette, posing for photographers from the horsey press. The type of show Dee entered would have those. Horsey press photographers didn't bother going to shows attended by the likes of Drummer and me.

"Mmmm, I wonder how poor old Mrs Collins is getting on," said Katy, looking through her red sweet wrapper at Bluey. "Oh, wow, Bluey looks fabulous as a strawberry roan. But then, he would," she added, totally besotted by her pony.

"Yes, poor Mrs C," agreed Bean.

Mrs Collins was our ponies' landlady and, as I've mentioned, she lived alone in her house on the yard. Except that she wasn't living there at the moment because only a week ago she'd been carted off to hospital in an ambulance after suffering a heart-attack. Sophie, Dee-Dee's mum, was looking after Mrs Collins's cats and greyhound, Squish, and we were all mucking in, glad to help. Old Mrs C was a bit batty but everyone was hoping she'd be back soon. I mean, she was OK really, and sometimes, almost sane.

"I think you ought to tell those two trespassers to clear off, James," said Katy, bossily.

"Well, it's strange but they don't look very lost,"

James replied. They look like they mean to be here. You go and tell them if you're that worried."

"I'm too comfortable," Katy snorted, "and you're a right wimp! Here, Bean," she waved the sweet wrapper in Bean's direction, "see what Tiffany looks like pink."

"No thanks, I like her all golden and gorgeous. I'll go and tell them," Bean volunteered, getting to her feet and stretching. Nearby, Drummer and Bambi lifted their heads from grazing, still chewing as they watched Bean walk across the field towards the gate where the two strangers were standing.

I could imagine the conversation: Bean would politely ask them whether they were lost. They would nod their heads and ask where the mislaid footpath was. Bean would point to the next field. They would thank her and head for the right path, avoiding the pony poo and climbing through the fence, turning to give Bean a wave of thanks. It happened now and again. I'd put walkers right before.

My gaze swung round to Drummer. He really is the most wonderful, fabulous bay pony. OK, he isn't the politest pony in the world (sometimes he's downright rude), but he has a heart of gold, even if he does hide it successfully. And there was Bambi standing next to him, as close as she could get, her muzzle resting on Drummer's mahogany back. I heard myself sigh. If we didn't come up with some sort of plan soon . . .

"There must be a way!" Katy insisted, as though able to hear my thoughts. She said it at least once a day. She'd been saying it at least once a day since Santa's busiest night of the year.

"Yes, there must," James agreed, exasperated, "but the trouble is, we don't know what it is!"

"Yet!" I said, determined to be positive.

"Let's go through it again . . ." began Katy. James groaned and my heart sank, too. We didn't need to spell it out again, we knew *what* we had to do, we just didn't know *how* to do it.

"There *has* to be a way!" Katy said again, scratching her head, determined that if she said it enough times, the answer would present itself to her. It hadn't yet. Her red hair was caught back in a band – purple of course, she never seemed to wear any other colour. James had once asked her, in mock seriousness, whether she thought she would grow out of purple and graduate to, say, green or blue. Katy had just stared at him as though he was mad.

"Yes, there is a way, Katy," James said, "we're just waiting for you to tell us what it is. So what is it?"

Katy screwed up her sweet wrapper and threw it at James.

"Ahhhh!" screamed James dramatically, his hand flying upwards and covering one side of his face. "My eye, my eye!"

For a second, Katy looked appalled then, realising she'd been had, gave James a shove. "Very funny!" she said. "NOT!" she added.

Bean hurried back across the field. She looked a lot less relaxed than she had when she'd left us. Something wasn't right. I looked over to the gate, the man and the woman were still there, looking around them and writing something down in a notebook.

"What's up?" asked James, noticing Bean's expression. She flopped down beside us and tore at the grass, her eyebrows knotting together in a frown under her blonde fringe. "Weren't they grateful to be shown the right path?

"They're not hikers," said Bean, chewing her lip.

"Then why were they looking at a map?" asked Katy.

"It wasn't a map," gulped Bean.

"Who are they then?" I asked.

"The man said his name was Robert Collins. He said he was Mrs Collins's son."

"I didn't know she had any family," said Katy, sitting up, "she never said."

We stared at the strangers with renewed interest, fixating on the man, Mrs Collins's son.

"I've never seen him before," added James.

"Well, that's what he said," Bean, shrugging her shoulders. Her voice was all wobbly.

"So what's he doing here? Now?" Katy asked her.

Bean sniffed. James edged closer and put his arm around her shoulders, sparking pangs of jealousy in my heart. I only hoped James would never find out about my unrequited feelings for him.

"What is it, Bean, why are you so upset? What did they say to you?" he asked gently.

"They said . . ." began Bean, "Robert Collins said . . ." she stopped.

I felt my heart skip a beat for a different reason. Whatever had Mrs Collins's son said to upset Bean so much?

Bean gulped. "He told me that he was selling Laurel Farm for development." Bean started crying. "The paper was covered in plans for new houses in this very field, and he said that we would all have to find new homes for the ponies!"

Chapter Two

We wasted no time setting off alarm bells with everyone else who was at the yard that day.

"Are you absolutely certain, Bean, that's what he said?" asked Nicky, leading her daughter Bethany around the yard on their ancient and tiny bay pony, Pippin. "I mean," she added, giving everyone a knowing look, "you do sometimes get the wrong end of the stick, don't you?"

"We all went and talked with Robert-blinking-Collins," James told her, defending Bean. "He confirmed it. He told us that Mrs C isn't able to look after herself any more and that she'll be going into a home."

"And he's selling the land to a developer," interrupted Katy, "who's going to build hundreds of houses on the field!"

14

The field where Drummer and his friends grazed, I thought. I looked over Nicky's shoulder to the field and the outdoor arena where we all schooled the ponies, and imagined buildings covering the grass.

"It's a prime site," James said, echoing Robert Collins's words. "Houses will sell like hot cakes around here."

"He didn't seem very upset about his mum," Bean said. Her eyes were still red where she'd been crying.

"Aren't we sitting tenants or something?" asked Katy. "He can't just chuck us all out, can he?"

"Perhaps we should have a sit-in. You know, stop the development, make banners, petition parliament or something," I suggested, imagining us all lined up on the drive facing up to big yellow bulldozers.

"Great idea!" enthused Katy, her eyes flashing. "We can RIDE to parliament on the ponies. That will get the press behind us."

"Tiffany's lethal in traffic," mumbled Bean.

"Slow down," said James, holding up his hands. "Oh, good, here's Sophie, she always knows what to do."

Sophie's gigantic horsebox trundled past us, a red, blue and tri-colour champion rosette fluttering in the cab, flanked by a red and a blue. It had been a good day, I thought. And we were about to spoil it, big time.

We all followed in its wake, waiting impatiently for Sophie to park and turn off the engine. Dee-Dee jumped down from the cab.

"You all look well gloomy," she said. Her cream showing shirt was crumpled and the front of it hung outside her butter-coloured showing jodhpurs. She'd replaced her boots with trainers, her brown hair was scooped up in a grip and she had a smudge on one cheek and what looked like chocolate around her mouth. "What's up?"

We all explained in a jumble of words and Dee and her mum listened aghast. When we'd finished, and Sophie had got to the bottom of all the gabble of explanations, she pressed her lips together and frowned.

"Hmmmm," she murmured. "Is this Robert Collins person still here?"

"No," I told her. "He drove off half-an-hour ago. The woman went with him. She was a surveyor or something."

"Hmmmm," Sophie said again. "And Mrs C is going into a home?"

"That's what he said," gulped Bean. "Poor Mrs C. She'll hate it in a home. Who will look after the cats? Who'll have Squish?"

"Slow down, Bean," Sophie told her. "I went to see Mrs Collins in hospital yesterday and she didn't say anything about going into a home."

We all looked at her, appalled.

"You mean she doesn't know?" asked Katy. "That's terrible!"

"Well, things could have changed," Sophie told us, "but when I saw her she was talking about getting one of those stair lifts in her house – she said she was always a bit puffed whenever she climbed the stairs. She never said anything about her son, or building on the land."

"So her devoted son – not – has big plans he's neglected to tell her," James said grimly.

We were all quiet. How horrible, I thought. Could relatives do things like that? Surely Mrs C would have something to say about it. She wasn't exactly a shrinking violet. But, of course, one never knew how people behaved with their family and Robert Collins looked a bit meaty. I imagined him intimidating Mrs C – she was only tiny – shouting and making her sign papers. I shuddered.

"Let me make some more enquiries," Sophie suggested. "If this were to happen, we would all have to be given a month's notice to leave . . ."

"A month!" I said, dismayed. Could we all really have to go in a month?

"It's in your contract," Sophie said. I realised I hadn't read mine properly when I'd come to Laurel Farm. All that small print – boring. Now it seemed very important indeed.

"But Mum, we can't just all go!" wailed Dee, waving her arms about.

"Well yes, actually, we can if we have to," Sophie told her, matter-of-factly.

"*Where?*" Dee asked.

"There are plenty of other livery yards around here," said Sophie, calmly.

I stared into the distance. How awful to be the new girl again. I'd only just started to feel part of the gang here. And Drummer had made good friends – one very good friend – at last. The thought of moving physically hurt, I felt a pang in my stomach.

"Can't you tell Mrs Collins?" asked James.

"I could," agreed Sophie, "but I wouldn't like to just yet. She's still frail and she doesn't need any extra worry. This Robert Collins will need to get planning permission and that takes a while so I shouldn't think there is any need to panic – yet, anyway." She pressed her thumb to her lips, thinking. Unlike her daughter,

Sophie oozed sophistication in her immaculate breeches, shining long leather boots and a crisp white shirt. Her hair was caught back in a bun – she looked like she was about to go to the show, instead of coming back from it. I wondered whether Dolly had won the tri-coloured rosette, or Sophie's horse, Lester. Now didn't seem the time to ask.

"Although he could want us out before he applies for planning so there's nothing to stop him," Sophie continued. "Leave it with me," she told us. "I'll find out more. Nothing is going to happen yet – we haven't been given notice so don't worry too much before we know the facts. My friend Helena's husband is in the planning department, I'll give her a ring later to ask some questions. Now, Dee, we have to get Lester and Dolly out of the horsebox and settled in their stables. They've worked hard today. Come on!"

I hardly felt reassured. Sophie always knew someone who knew someone who was helpful for this and that and if anyone could find out what was going on, she could, but she hadn't given us any reason to suppose that we could actually do anything about the development. She had seemed almost resigned to moving. Perhaps it didn't matter as much to her where her horse was stabled. It was our gang that was threatened. I couldn't believe how, in an instant, our whole world had come tumbling down.

As Dee led Dolly down the ramp we all drifted away back towards the field and leant miserably on the fence. I could see Drummer. He was still eating. It was his favourite thing to do. How much longer would he be able to munch the grass at Laurel Farm?

"Mrs Bradley will be terribly upset to find somewhere new for Henry," I said, thinking of the elderly lady who kept her Dales pony at the yard.

"And Cat, she doesn't know yet," said Katy.

"It won't make any difference to Cat, will it," said James, gloomily, "due to our failure to come up with a plan."

Sadly, that was true. Maybe that was *why* we hadn't come up with a plan, because it would all have been pointless.

I straightened up. I couldn't hang around moping any longer. Only one person could make me feel better when I was feeling this low. The same person who was always there for me whatever crisis I was going through. The one person who always understood and totally got how I was feeling, and even though he didn't always seem to say the right thing at the time, it always turned out to be words of wisdom.

"I'm going to talk to Drummer," I announced.

"Shall we come?" Katy asked.

I shook my head. "No, no thanks. I think I'd rather it was just me and Drum. You don't mind, do you?"

Three heads shook slowly.

Drummer knew something was wrong, of course. He always does.

"What major catastrophe has occurred now?" he asked me as I wandered over.

Oh, sorry, with all this going on I forgot to explain how I can hear what Drummer says. Actually, I can hear what all horses and ponies say, provided I have my tiny stone statue – the one I keep in my pocket – of a Celtic goddess, name of Epona, with me. I found her when Drum and I first came to Laurel Farm: the area has a history of ancient Roman occupation and Epona was worshipped in Ancient Rome, too. But now I have her, and she somehow provides a translation service so that I can understand equine. No-one else knows about her (except for James, but he's been sworn to secrecy in return for borrowing Epona now and again so he can talk to Moth), and everyone else thinks I'm some kind of pony whisperer, so that's what I'm known as. It can be great – but it can also be a bit awkward. You know how some people can take things the wrong way or get

21

a bit funny about stuff they don't understand? Cat had been like that with me for ages.

The sun was still shining and warm, the birds were still singing and all the trees and bushes were stretching out of their spring blossom and into their summer foliage but the excitement I had felt earlier had gone. It had left with Robert Collins.

"In your own time," Drummer prompted me, as I struggled to find the words. So I told him all about the latest bombshell – to add to his other worries. But then, as James had said, being given notice to leave Laurel Farm wouldn't make any difference to Cat's problem, so the same applied to her pony Bambi, and Drummer, too.

"So have we all been told to go?" Drummer asked, getting to the heart of the matter and not bothering to ask pointless questions.

"No, not yet," I replied, twirling a lock of his black mane around my fingers. It was a comfort, somehow.

"And Sophie's on the case?"

"Yes. Sophie knows someone who might be able to advise us."

"If anyone can do something, Sophie can," said Drummer. "She's formidable."

My face cracked into a smile. Drum was right there,

I wouldn't have argued with Sophie. Formidable was exactly the right word for her. But even so . . .

"But she says we have to go if we're given notice," I said, remembering her words. "She can't stop the development."

"Then who can?" Drummer asked.

Who can? I thought about it. Who can stop the development? "I don't know," I replied, staring ahead of me and seeing nothing. That was the big question, who could stop the development? If we were the ones to be affected by it, then surely we had to stop it. Drummer had put his hoof on it – as usual. Bulldozers loomed in my mind again and then disappeared. No one would care whether we had to find new homes for the ponies, not when people needed somewhere to live themselves.

"I don't know who can stop it," I said, my mind whirling.

"Well, it seems to me that's what you need to find out," said Drummer, dropping his head again to pull at the grass. "Because," he continued, munching, "if you can get the building stopped, we can all stay and you can put your efforts into solving the most important problem, which you seem to have forgotten."

"But I don't know who can stop it!" I repeated,

confused by Drummer's warped sense of priorities. "And I haven't forgotten the other problem!"

"Well then, you need to take matters into your own hands and get it stopped yourself, don't you? And get a wiggle on!"

Chapter Three

"So now we have to come up with *two* plans!" announced Katy, as we all mounted up in the yard the next day.

"We haven't even come up with one, yet," Cat pointed out, tightening Bambi's girth from the saddle. Bambi snaked her head to and fro and snapped her teeth in protest. Cat's skewbald mare loved a bit of theatrics.

"Don't remind us!" Bean groaned, ignoring Tiffany's side-step past a perfectly innocent-looking broom.

"Let's go for a blast up the Sloping Field," James suggested, urging his chestnut mare Moth into a brisk walk towards the bridlepath. As usual, an Indian blanket replaced a conventional numnah under Moth's saddle and she lifted her white legs up high, her chin on her chest as James sat astride her in his ripped jeans, his stirrups too long. We all followed – all except Dee. She was hardly ever allowed to come hacking with us in the summer due to Sophie's conviction that Dolly would pick up bad manners from our out-of-control ponies. She had a point.

I still couldn't get used to riding with Cat. When I first came to Laurel Farm Cat had been my arch enemy but since we'd all practised and performed an activity ride at Christmas, things had been better between us – especially now I knew the big secret which had upset Cat so much and had made her behave so badly towards me. And now I knew, I could totally understand why it had made her go a bit, well, 'mad' is the only way I can describe it really, whenever it had cropped up. Now Cat knew of my determination to help her, she'd softened towards me. It sounds quite simple when I say it all like that, but it's really complicated.

For a start, even though I realise why Cat was horrible to me, I can't quite forgive her. I'm just relieved she isn't calling me Brighton any more and being all snarley at me. And there's the little matter of her having gone out with James. I can't quite get my head around that one. Not totally, even if James did have a perfectly good reason for asking her out.

Drummer has never let me forget how miffed I was about that.

Drummer, as usual, hurried along to be next to Bambi. Bambi was the reason we needed to come up with a plan because in July, Bambi was due to move out of Laurel Farm and into a single stable and paddock waiting for her at Cat's aunt's place. Because Cat's Aunt Pam is Bambi's real owner (that had been the big secret – I had always thought she belonged to Cat), and Cat had Bambi on loan while Aunt Pam had a couple of kids. Now the kids were old enough to ride Aunt Pam had announced her intention of repossessing her pony at the start of the school holidays, leaving my until-recently-arch-enemy Bambi-less.

So why have I vowed to think up a plan to save Cat's pony? Why should I care about my until-recently-arch-enemy when she has previously done all she could to diss me? (She even tried to get Drummer stolen once.) Because my wonderful Drummer and Bambi are an item and so loved-up it's touching (or sick-making, depending on your mood). Without a plan, they won't have much longer to make like a couple.

True, I could empathise with Cat (I couldn't imagine losing Drummer) but the real reason I was so anxious to come up with a plan to save Bambi was because of my pony. He loved Bambi. I couldn't, I wouldn't let him down. Everyone seemed to believe it was out of kindness to Cat that I was so anxious to help. After all, no-one else could hear what Drummer, or any of the other ponies said, without Epona.

"So let's recap on ideas we have come up with for the *Keep Bambi Campaign*," suggested Katy, giving her beloved Bluey's blue-flecked neck a loving pat. Bluey arched his neck and looked pleased. He loves Katy as much as she loves him.

"The ones we've already rejected?" I asked.

"Yes. We may be able to convert them into a workable plan, or amalgamate a couple of them to get something that does work."

"Well, there's the 'Hide Bambi at the ice house' plan," said Bean.

"I don't rate that one," I heard Bambi say. She'd had a bad experience at the ice house once before.

"She can't stay there forever," Cat pointed out.

"And even if she did, she'd still be in solitary," said James. "The idea is to keep her not only with Cat but with all the other ponies at Laurel Farm."

"If Laurel Farm still exists," I pointed out, gloomily.

"We're addressing that issue later," Katy declared firmly.

"I still think we ought to try to raise some money to buy her," said Bean. "That's the best idea yet."

"That would be brilliant – except that my Aunt Pam doesn't want to *sell* Bambi," Cat reminded us all, "she wants her *back*."

"Would you be able to keep her if you could buy her?" asked Katy.

Cat nodded. "My family pays for her keep now," she explained. "But they can't afford the money up front to buy a pony. When Bambi goes, that's it, I'm pony-less."

"Don't forget Dee's idea," I said, waiting for the inevitable response.

Everyone groaned.

"No séances!" cried Katy, making Tiffany jump.

"That's Dee's answer to everything," mumbled James.

"Exactly when did you all hold a séance?" asked Cat. She asked it every time the subject came up. Nobody wanted to tell her because it had happened when we'd been competing against her and memories were not especially warm – for anyone. The idea had been to call up Dee's dear departed granddad but instead we'd got some nutter called Adam Rowe who had just wanted to spell out *bad death* all the time. Nice! It had been totally scary and we'd all been freaked out – except for

James, which only made us more convinced that he'd been pushing the beaker round and spelling out the words himself for a laugh. Some laugh!

"I thought the *Let's find a more suitable pony for AP's kids* plan was a good idea," interrupted James, anxious to move on from the séance subject.

"Yes, apart from us not having any money to buy one. And AP, as you like to call my Aunt Pam," Cat said, "as we've already established, wants her beloved Bambi back, not just any old pony. It's a no go!"

We all pulled up at the bottom of the Sloping Field and I could feel Drummer start to bunch underneath me in anticipation. All the ponies knew that the Sloping Field meant only one thing: a flat-out gallop from the bottom to the top with the added fun of a leap across the stream which snaked its way across the middle. I could hear all the ponies winding each other up – Bambi and Drummer were already challenging each other to a race.

"See ya . . ." Bean told us as Tiffany leapt into the air and hit the ground at the gallop, totally oblivious to Bean's wishes. James leant forward to give Moth the go and Drummer pulled the reins out of my hands as he stuck his head down and went for it, neck-and-neck with Bambi. Only Bluey, well-mannered, polite Bluey, set off at a canter for Katy before easing gently into a gallop. James overtook Bean half-way up the field and Bambi and Drummer reached the top in a dead heat because neither of them wanted to beat the other (see what I mean about sick-making?).

We all stood at the top of the field and looked around at the countryside while the ponies got their breath back. No wonder the Romans had settled here, I thought, drinking in the view. No wonder there had been large houses built around here for centuries after the invaders had sailed back home to the warmth of their native Italy. It seemed strange to think of so many generations of people all looking down from more-or-less where we all stood now, all seeing – give or take a few trees – the same view as ours on this beautiful May morning.

"Did anyone hear that?" asked Tiffany, lifting her head, her ears twitching.

All the other ponies groaned.

"You need to get the vet to look at your ears," Bambi told her.

"It's my nerves," Tiffany explained.

"*Your* nerves get on *my* nerves," Drummer told her, and he and Bambi put their heads together and sniggered.

"OK," said James, loosening Moth's reins so she could stretch her neck, "now we need to think about this other little concern we have, namely, the proposed development at Laurel Farm."

"Sophie's friend's husband has confirmed that we can't do anything legally," sighed Katy.

"But we have to stop the development," I said. The thought of moving to another yard now, when Drum and I had made friends at Laurel Farm, was too much to bear.

"How, exactly?" Cat asked, dropping Bambi's reins and fiddling with the strap on her riding hat. "We can't even come up with any workable ideas for the *Keep Bambi Campaign*."

"Well, we're the only people who will care enough to get it stopped," I said, remembering Drummer's words. "If we don't do anything, we'll lose Laurel Farm. No-one else will bother."

"SOS, that's what it is," said Katy. "Save Our Stables! There, that's the name of our new campaign."

"We'll have more campaigns than Napoleon at this rate," remarked James.

"Isn't he dead?" asked Bean, confused.

"If he wasn't we could tap him up for some ideas," mused Katy.

"Thank goodness Dee isn't here," I said. "She'd be all for calling up Napoleon on the ouija board."

"Oh please no," groaned Bean, "I can't speak French!"

"Can you all do me a favour," yelled Cat, her green eyes flashing, "Either fill me in on the séance story or just shut up about it!"

"Do you think anyone else will care?" asked Bean, moving the subject on hastily. "About Laurel Farm, I mean, not the sé . . .," she looked across at Cat and changed her mind, ". . . the S word."

"Not really," said James. "Laurel Farm is just one of lots of stables in this area, I can't see anyone bothering about it, they'll just say we can take the ponies elsewhere. Besides, not many people know Laurel Farm even exists, it's so well hidden from the road. They're not likely to miss it."

"Poor Mrs Collins," said Bean.

"Yeah," agreed Cat, "I bet she's feeling wretched. She won't want to go into some home and lose the stables, not to mention her cats and Squish."

"But it sounds like she doesn't even know about her son's plans," Katy reminded us.

Drummer edged towards a bush and tried to eat it. "Let's go into the woods," I suggested. "We might find some inspiration there."

We didn't. It was nice though, all damp-smelling and mossy underfoot, dappled sunlight finding its way through the trees. A few weeks before, the ground had been smothered with bluebells.

"We need to get some media coverage," said Katy, her purple hoodie swaying in time to Bluey's footsteps.

"What, the papers and the telly?" asked Bean.

"Exactly!" Katy said.

"We need a friendly celebrity to be on our side," said James.

"Like who?"

"No idea, but it would have to be someone sympathetic to ponies," James pointed continued. "I mean, most people think anyone with horses is so well-off, they can afford their own land. It's not like our ponies are going to be put down or anything if the development goes through."

"Shhhh," hissed Bean, dropping her reins and leaning forward to cover Tiffany's ears with her hands. Seized by panic, Tiffany put her head down and shook it so violently, Bean slid down her neck on to the ground.

"Whoops, my fault," said Bean, rolling over and getting to her feet.

"Sorry," said Tiffany, even though Bean couldn't hear

her. "I thought you were an ear-grabbing monster. Give me some warning next time."

We all waited for Bean to re-mount. It took a bit of time because although she is tall and willowy in stature, she has virtually no spring.

"So what sort of story does the media like?" I asked, watching Bean haul herself up by Tiffany's saddle. If my old riding instructor had seen her she'd have had a complete nut-do on the spot.

"Sensational sob stories," said James, "with celebrity endorsement!"

"What, like the ponies would all die of broken hearts if they were split up, that sort of thing?" asked Cat.

"Well they will," I said, stroking Drummer's neck. "Drum and Bambi should never be parted."

"Absolutely!" snorted Drummer.

"Try telling other people that," said James.

"Do you think that would work?" asked Bambi – but I was the only one who could hear her.

"Some people will care," snapped Cat. She and James were still not quite back to being totally civil to each other since they'd been out together. It hadn't ended well. James had chucked Cat so the atmosphere was still a bit tense between them.

"How about telling them about Mrs Collins?" asked

Bean, back in the saddle again. "She shouldn't be made homeless because of some development."

"It's not like her son is throwing her out on the street," I said. "She's going into a home. Lots of people go into a home."

"Even if they don't want to," Bean mumbled.

"I can't see a story, then," Katy sighed. "If only we knew someone in TV or who worked on the papers, they might be able to see an angle."

"Pia's been on TV," Bean reminded everyone.

"I don't know anyone though," I said. I'd been on TV twice: once on an afternoon chat show with some big-wig horse experts and the second time in a one-off special with just me called *Pony Whispering Live!* It didn't exactly make me in with the lovey set.

We set off for home, the ponies quickening pace as they knew they'd get a feed and turned out in the field once we got back to the yard. All of us were in a sombre mood – the ride had produced absolutely no ideas, no solutions. It was mega depressing.

"I can't bear the thought of all these lovely old farm buildings being torn down for new houses," Bean wailed as we rode along the drive.

"They'll probably convert them, people go mad for converted farm buildings, especially barns," James told her. "There'll be a trendy couple living in the stables now inhabited by Dolly, Tiff and Bluey, and Moth, Bambi and Drum's row will be converted into a car port for their 4X4s and sporty little numbers."

"Stop it, James!" squealed Bean, putting her hands over her own ears this time.

We all fed, brushed off and turned out the ponies before going our separate ways. I cycled home part of the way with Bean, peeling off at the crossroads towards the tiny cottage which is home for me and my mum. A shiny red motorbike was parked outside, which could only mean one thing . . .

Chapter Four

"Anybody home?" I yelled, banging the front door. I so didn't want my mum and her motorbike-riding boyfriend *not* to know I was about to barge in on them. But it was all right, they were sitting entwined around each other on the sofa, eating chocolates in front of a blazing fire and watching the TV. Mum had been going out with Mike-the-bike for almost seven months now. A record. I was relieved. Mike-the-bike was fairly normal compared to most of my mum's dates – some of them had been well weird and definitely, definitely not sticking-around-material. Nicking a chocolate, I flopped down on the chair and pulled a face.

"It's warm outside," I said, "why the fire?"

"It's romantic," said Mike, giving Mum a look which plainly said that was how she saw it. He looked a bit hot.

My mum slapped his arm and pulled a face at him. "No brainwaves about how to stop the development yet?" she asked, sucking the chocolate off a brazil nut before spitting it out into the palm of her hand and throwing it into the fire where it shrivelled up with a hiss.

"What a waste!" I exclaimed.

"You could have had it!" joked Mike, aiming a grin in my direction.

"That's gross!" I replied, totally taking the bait. Mum just shrugged her shoulders and flicked back her blonde hair. I could remember a time when she was always putting on airs to impress boyfriends. Thank goodness she was over that phase with Mike.

"No good wasting good chocolate," she said, "and I hate brazil nuts."

I decided to ignore her. "No, we can't think of a single way to initiate our Save Our Stables campaign," I told them, miserably.

"You want to get someone famous to help you," said Mike, yawning.

"That's what James said," I told him.

"Something will come up," said Mike, rather optimistically, I thought.

"What's for dinner?" I asked, suddenly starving.

"Omelette and salad," Mum told me.

"What a cop-out," I moaned.

"You can get it yourself if you take that attitude," Mum replied, digging out another chocolate and throwing it into her mouth. "Oh yeuk," she said, pulling a face, "coffee creme. I'd rather eat a brazil nut!"

"That's karma!" I replied, dodging the cushion she threw at me.

I went upstairs to change. As I threw my waistcoat on to the bed Epona fell out on to the floor and I bent down to pick her up. The tiny stone statue of the Celtic-come-Roman goddess sitting sideways on her tiny horse felt rough to the touch.

"It's hard to imagine you're so old," I told her rudely, rubbing my thumb across her face where her nose used to be. It was her only damage, apart from 2,000 years worth of (not much) wear and tear. I wondered who she had belonged to, what Roman cavalryman had held her in his hand as I held her now, and how he had worshipped her. It was a strange thought. Epona was the Celtic goddess of horses, I remembered, my mind working overtime. Well, it couldn't hurt, I thought.

Placing Epona on my dressing table I sat solemnly in front of her, wondering if I had lost all my marbles. I decided it was still worth a try, if only for Drummer's sake. I was getting desperate.

"Epona," I said, in my most humble voice, "we need your help. The ponies need your help. You're supposed to look after them,' (that sounded a bit accusing, I thought, but it was too late to take it back), 'so please, please can you help us save Bambi and Laurel Farm? We've tried to think of something ourselves, but we just can't. Please help us."

Nothing happened, of course. I didn't get a blinding burst of inspiration. No grand plan slammed into my head. Epona just sat there silently in her familiar, ancient, stone way and I felt rather stupid. But then an idea did whoosh into my brain (and who could say that Epona hadn't put it there?). Didn't the Ancient Romans make *sacrifices* to their gods? I wondered what sort of sacrifice I could make. Slaughtering some animal was way, way out, of course and I couldn't think of anything I owned which might be worth something. I had no jewellery, no antique furniture. I couldn't even think of anything I owned that I particularly valued, even if it wasn't actually worth money. That was what sacrifices were all about, weren't they? What did I have that I most valued?

Looking around my room my eyes zoomed immediately to my most treasured possessions – the rosettes and sash I'd won at Hickstead in the Sublime Equine Team Challenge, my beautiful blue sash which I had always, always dreamed of winning. I remembered how I'd felt when it had been presented to me and Drummer, how proud I had been, how elated I had felt galloping around the famous arena wearing it, just like the top show jumpers.

I felt my heart beating in my chest – it was as though my whole body was throbbing. I felt as though my heart was in my ears, thumping away like a drum.

Drum.

Drummer.

Which was more important to me, some ribbons or my pony? No contest. Besides, it was Drum who had won the sash for me and, whatever happened, I would always remember the day when we'd won it. No one could ever take the memory away, my feeling of pride, my absolute joy. Those feelings could never be lost, never be sacrificed.

Without allowing myself time to think about it I leapt up on to my bed, ripped my beautiful blue sash with its silver writing from the wall and pausing only to throw Epona a pleading glance and show her what I held in my arms, I ran downstairs, bursting through the sitting room door to see Mum and Mike turn towards me in surprise. Without meeting their eyes or pausing to give myself a chance to think again I hurled my prized Hickstead sash into the fire where it immediately burst into flames with a crackle and hiss.

Mum was on her feet in a second, looking at me in bewilderment. "What on earth are you doing?" she shrieked, seizing the fire tongs and lifting the shrinking and spitting sash already engulfed by orange and red flames. "That's your Hickstead sash, Pia!" she cried, like I didn't know.

"Leave it, let it burn!" I implored her, "and please, please don't ask me why!" I added, turning to gallop back up to my room, failing to fight back the tears.

It's only a bit of old ribbon, I told myself, throwing myself on to my bed and sobbing. It's not a sacrifice if it doesn't mean anything. That's what a sacrifice is all about.

"Pia, are you all right, love?" It was Mum, tapping on my door.

"I'm OK, Mum, honest," I managed to say, between gulps. "I just want to be left alone."

I heard her go back downstairs. She was great at giving me space. After Dad had run off with Skinny Lynny she knew the value of working through things alone. I rolled over and even though I didn't want to, I looked up at the wall. Even with the three beautiful rosettes still hanging there it looked empty. The hole where my beautiful sash had, until moments ago, been hanging seemed vast. Rummaging around in the cupboard I pulled out a poster of a beautiful black horse and stuck it in the gaping hole. It didn't look right. It didn't look right at all. Nothing could ever replace a Hickstead sash, so desperately coveted, so hard won.

Through my tears I could see Epona still sitting on my dressing table where I'd left her and I stared at her for signs that my sacrifice hadn't been in vain. There were none. Reminding myself of why I had done something so reckless I gazed at the pictures of Drummer littered around my bedroom. His happiness was worth so much more than a sash, I knew that. As was staying with our new friends, I had to keep remembering that, too.

Eventually the tears dried up, leaving me with bloodshot eyes and a face that looked like a balloon. Poo. I'd have to face the inevitable questions downstairs at some point and I didn't even have a credible story to tell, the truth sounded so ridiculous. Even Mum doesn't know about Epona.

Sighing, I put my stone statue back in my waistcoat pocket and went downstairs for dinner.

Chapter Five

When I got to the yard the next day the first thing I
saw was a trail of water from where Lester, Pippin and
Henry's stables were, oozing around the corner on to
Drummer's part of the yard like a silvery, shimmering,
growing snake. Cursing whoever had left the hose on
I pedalled my bike around the corner only to find
Bean bending over the tap, her blonde hair soaked
and dripping.

"Whatever are you doing?" I asked her.

Bean did a really good Tiffany impersonation,
leaping in the air and gasping.

"Oh, don't just appear like that!" she gasped,
clutching her chest.

"What am I supposed to do," I asked, "send you
a letter?"

Bean stuck her head under the hose again.

"What," I repeated, "are you doing?"

Inclining her head sideways, Bean dropped the hose and reached for the bottle of shampoo resting on an upturned bucket.

"What does it look like I'm doing?" she replied, like *I* was the strange one. "I'm washing my hair."

"With Tiffany's shampoo?" I asked, recognising the bottle.

"It's for palominos," said Bean, like that explained it. "*I'm* a palomino."

"Isn't the water, like, freezing?"

"Yeah, it is but the sun's warm and it'll dry really quickly."

"Want some of Drummer's conditioner?" I asked her. "It makes his tail silky-soft."

"Oooh yeah, thanks," Bean replied, rinsing soapy water all over the yard.

I fetched the conditioner from Drum's tackbox and watched as Bean massaged it into her hair. Once it was rinsed out (with a gasp at the temperature of the water), Bean rubbed her head in one of Tiffany's towels before combing her hair through with a mane comb.

"That feels so much better," she said, her teeth chattering.

"You're bonkers," I told her. "Why didn't you wash it at home?"

"Everyone had used all the hot water," Bean said, running her fingers through her hair to get it to dry.

"Do you want to think about that for a moment?" I asked her, unable to fathom her logic. "You really are bonkers, you know!"

James walked by with Moth's headcollar, headed for the field. Looking at Bean combing her wet hair, then at me, he shook his head. He'd given up trying to fathom Bean.

"Wait for me," I said, running back to get Drummer's headcollar, "I'll come with you and get Drummer in."

We walked side-by-side to the field, going through the gate and past Pippin, who was grazing nearby, over to the far side of the field where the rest of the ponies were trying to make out they weren't there.

"Hey Drummer!" I called.

Drummer looked over to me and yawned. No way was he going to make an effort and meet me halfway. He was going to make me walk all the way over to catch him. Moth at least showed willing, taking a step or two forward for James.

Thanks for showing me up, Drum, I thought. You're

a pal. I threw my Hickstead sash in the fire for you and you can't even be bothered to wander over.

"You know, Pia, I think what you are doing for Cat totally rocks," James said.

I suddenly felt a bit hot. "Er, how do you mean?" I asked.

"Well, everybody knows how Cat has always been mean to you," James continued. "She even tried to get Drummer stolen once, didn't she?"

"Yeah, well," I mumbled, unwilling to revisit that episode.

"The way you're so determined to help Cat keep Bambi, and got everyone to think up ideas as well, I'm a bit in awe of you, to tell the truth," James went on, making it worse.

"Um, well, I just know how I would feel if it was happening to Drummer and me," I mumbled.

"I think it's noble," said James, offering Moth a carrot and putting on her headcollar. "You're bigger than I would be if I were in your shoes," he continued. "Lend us *You-know-who* for a while, will you? I haven't spoken to Moth for ages."

Digging Epona out of my pocket I handed her over. James borrowed her now and again to keep up to speed with his pony. She was the only pony who refused to

49

talk to me, due to her mistrust of humans in general, but she did talk to James, via our Roman-goddess-interpreter, of course. It seemed a fair trade for James's silence about Epona. Who was I kidding? It was great to share a secret together. It was the only relationship we did have, after all.

My feelings of elation following James's glowing words were gradually replaced by the knowledge that I was a real sham. I was taking the credit for something that simply wasn't true.

"To tell the truth", James had said. The phrase rattled around my brain. I had felt pretty tra-la-la when James had bigged me up – but for something I didn't deserve and that he'd totally misinterpreted? I didn't think so. Noble, he'd said. I didn't feel noble. Luckily, without Epona, I was spared Drummer's take on our conversation. He was bound to have something to say about it and it wouldn't be good.

My conscience bothered me. I'd had an opportunity to come clean with James but I'd passed that opportunity by. I'd let him think my motives for helping Cat keep Bambi were unselfish. I'd allowed him to big me up and give me credit for something that wasn't true.

I wasn't helping Catriona for Catriona's sake. I'd

often thought about how I would feel if she and Bambi were no longer at Laurel's Farm. How peaceful it would be for me, how I would no longer have to worry about her snide remarks and name-calling and I had to admit, it had sounded more than a good idea from my point of view. OK, she had been better since the activity ride, but who knew how long that would last? We weren't exactly friends. Our relationship was one of mutual tolerance, rather than any real warmth.

The real and only reason I was desperate to find a solution to Cat's problem was because of Drummer's love for Bambi.

And now I had let James think it was because I was noble. I was anything but.

I brushed Drummer over and saddled him up. We hadn't had a schooling session for ages and now seemed as good a time as any. James gave me Epona back as I rode Drummer to the outdoor school. Immediately, I wished he hadn't.

"Boring!" moaned Drum, dragging his hooves.

"Oh be fair!" I replied, "we haven't been out here for absolutely ages!"

"I'd hoped you'd given up schooling for the summer."

"No."

We walked and trotted around to warm up and then I asked Drum for some transitions, trying to get them absolutely spot on as we passed the markers. The first few were just OK, then we got a bit better, but then worse again, which was annoying. I decided to try some shallow loops and a few serpentines. These didn't go so well either.

OK, I thought, I'll have a go at perfecting our halts. It was something we weren't very good at – Drummer always seemed to take another step or two and leave a hind leg behind rather than standing square, and I was rubbish at correcting him.

Steering Drummer down the centre line I asked him to halt at X, at the very centre, concentrating on feeling my seat bones and hips. Were they level? My right hip felt slightly lower than my left, which meant Drummer had left his off hind behind. I nudged him with my right leg, but instead of bringing his off hind up underneath him, Drummer sighed and felt like a deflated balloon.

"What's the matter?" I asked him, leaning forward.

Drummer's ears went out sideways. "Oh, well, I think I'm depressed," he mumbled.

I jumped off and went to his head. "It's only a bit of schooling," I told him.

"Oh, it's not that," Drummer replied, hanging his head, "it's the Bambi thing. I don't know what I'll do if I lose her."

"Oh Drummer," I said, aghast. This wasn't like Drum. Usually he helped me whenever I was feeling down. Now I felt like I had nothing to say to him. No words of comfort. To make it worse, he lifted his head on to my shoulder and sighed again.

"Don't let her go," I heard him whisper.

I gulped and put my arms around his neck.

"I won't," I whispered back, "I promise." We stayed like that for a while and I had never felt so close to my pony – or so helpless. I was saying the right thing, but could I fulfil my promise?

"Can we go back in?" Drummer asked. "I really don't feel up to this."

"You don't usually let things get to you," I said, gently.

"Yeah, well, I'm a look-on-the-bright-side sort of pony," Drummer mumbled.

Really? I thought, saying nothing.

We walked back to the yard.

"That was quick!" exclaimed Bean.

I didn't feel I could explain so I just shrugged my shoulders and unsaddled Drummer, washing his bit under the tap before putting it away. I felt a bit depressed, too. It was catching, I thought, turning Drummer out again so he could be with Bambi. If he was feeling down, there was no point in doing anything else. I watched him canter over to her and they nuzzled each other before settling down to graze side-by-side.

I wandered back to the yard. I could see Katy rummaging around in the tackroom and Cat was in the barn. I decided I would weed the yard – it was looking a bit tatty.

Suddenly, James burst on to the scene from around the corner like some kind of comic book hero – without the stupid costume, obviously.

"Where is everyone?" he yelled, like we were hiding them.

"Er, well, Katy's grooming Bluey and . . ." Bean began.

"I've got it!" shouted James, punching the air so that his slightly-too long blonde hair fell over his eyes.

"Got what?" I asked him, trying not to notice his hair. It always does things to me so I try not to think about it. It's virtually impossible.

"The Stables SOS!" he said, "I know how we're going to save Laurel Farm!"

Chapter Six

"It's not about us!" explained James. "It's about *history*!"

Bean and I both looked at him blankly. I was beginning to think everyone was bonkers today. Except me, of course.

"You said it would be a shame if these farm buildings were pulled down," James said to Bean.

"Yeah, it would. Tiffany lives in one of them," Bean agreed. "Although I'd get her out first, obviously."

"I thought you said they wouldn't be?" said Katy. "You said they'd be turned into houses and car ports."

"Are these buildings important, then?" I asked, looking at the stables. They didn't look especially important. They were wooden, old and a bit ramshackle.

"Probably not," James said. "Why is your hair wet, Bean?" he added abruptly.

Bean, Katy and I exchanged glances. James wasn't

making sense and we didn't just mean about Bean's hair.

"But what about the house?" asked James, waving his arms around and jumping up and down.

"What, Mrs Collins's house?" asked Bean, frowning uncertainly as she glanced at the rather boring-looking brick built house next to the tackroom.

James looked as though he wanted to give Bean a shake. Usually, I know how he feels but I didn't think it was Bean who was being annoying this time.

"No, the *big* house!" yelled James. "The big house that used to be next to Laurel Farm."

The light went on in my brain. Honestly, sometimes it takes a while. I'd remembered James talking about the big house before, a huge house to which the farm belonged.

"But isn't that near the ice house?" I asked him. I had always assumed it had been. The ice house, where ice was taken from the lake to be stored all winter to be used in the summer at the big house, was over the other side of the bridlepath, on the other side of the lake. That was nowhere near the stables.

"Nah!" James said, all dismissive. "The ice house had to be near the water, but the house was here, in the ponies' field."

"I thought that was something you just made up," said Bean. "Was there really a house here?"

"Yep!" said James, nodding smugly.

"But it's not here any more," I said. "You told me there was no trace of it."

"But it's probably still a site of historical interest," James told us. "Some archaeological types would go mad for the chance to find out about it. And if that's so, the site is probably important, and planning permission would be refused."

"That sounds a bit, er, well, easy," said Katy.

"It's worth a try, isn't it?" yelled James.

"Yes," I said, nodding my head, "it certainly is!"

"What is?" asked Dee, appearing as if by magic.

In a jumble of words we all told her.

Dee's face lit up. "That totally is the way to go!" she said. "Good one, James. Now what do we do?"

"Let's go and take a look around and see if we can see anything," James suggested, and we all galloped into the field, our eyes on the grass.

"Where was it, exactly?" asked Dee. "Why is your hair damp, Bean? It hasn't been raining, has it?"

"Er, not really sure," mumbled James, striding away from the gate. "Big houses were usually built to take advantage of a view."

"So we have to decide where we would build a house, if we were going to," said Katy.

"Brilliant, Katy!" said Bean, fluffing up her hair in the sun.

"The highest ground is over here," I said, running to the hill and looking down at the villages below. You certainly could see for miles.

The ponies wandered over, curious as to what we were doing. They were on the make, of course.

"Got any treats?" Drummer asked me, frisking my pockets. He seemed to have perked up a bit now he was back with Bambi.

I shook my head. "No, but I've got something much more exciting – we think we've found a way to save the stables!"

All the ponies pricked up their ears. I explained that we were looking for the house which had been built so long ago.

"You're looking in the wrong place," said Bambi, gazing over to the left of us and not even bothering to look up. "It was over there, where that patch of long grass is by the hedge."

I blinked. "What did you just say?"

Bambi sighed impatiently. "It was over there!" she repeated, nodding her head in the direction.

"She's right," Drummer said. "It was definitely over there. Come on, we'll show you."

"Hold on!" I cried, holding up my hands. "How do you know?"

James, Katy, Dee and Bean all looked over. "What's up?" asked James.

"The ponies know where the house was," I told them. I guessed their faces mirrored mine. I mean, how on earth . . . ?

"Not difficult," explained Drummer, "if you're a pony. The ground gives off all sorts of vibes we can feel — which you can't. You'd be amazed at what the ground tells us that escapes you. To be honest, you're pretty useless. I don't know how you all get by."

"No wonder I'm of slightly nervous disposition," murmured Tiffany.

"*Slightly*?" I muttered.

"So where was it?" asked James, who had learned not to question what I told him from the ponies' mouths.

We trailed behind the ponies to the far side of the field.

Drummer stamped a front hoof and sniffed the ground. "Here, this is where the oldest one was built."

"Are you sure?" asked Katy. "There's no view from here." She turned accusingly to James. "I thought you

59

said it would have been built where the owners would have had a view."

Far from being able to see down the hill from this part of the field, all we could see were trees. There was no view at all.

"Excuse me," said Bluey – he really was a polite pony – "but those trees probably weren't there when the house was built."

Of course!

"When was the house built, James?" I asked.

"Originally? About four or five hundred years ago, according to Mrs Collins," James replied.

"Oh, that one," said Drummer, walking a bit to the left, "that's here."

"What do you mean, *that one*?" I asked. "How many are there?"

"Oh, loads!" he replied.

"Loads? How many is loads?"

"You're looking for the 400-year-old one – you did say that, didn't you?" asked Drum.

I nodded, dumbly.

"Then that's here," finished Drummer.

"Drummer seems to think there's more than one house," I told the others.

"Yeah," nodded James, "I think another house was

built when that one fell down, or something."

I was confused. I've never been very good with dates and things at school. "So which one *are* you talking about?" I asked Drummer.

"Well, the 400-year-old job, give or take a few years, that's under here," Drummer assured me.

"But that makes it . . ." began Dee, counting on her fingers, ". . . Elizabethan!"

"That alone justifies those huge fees your parents pay for your posh schooling Dee – pretty amazing, huh?" said James.

I pictured ladies wearing long dresses and stiff white ruffs around their necks, walking where we were now with men sporting more ruffs and pointed beards. A shiver ran up and down my spine. How strange to think of people all those years ago wandering over the same soil, looking at the same view.

"No wonder there's nothing left," said Bean, interrupting my thoughts.

"What's going on?" said a voice. It was Cat. In our excitement we'd failed to notice her arrival. "Why are you all bouncing about in the field? Your hair looks nice, Bean."

"James has the most amazing plan to save the stables!" Katy told her, and explained all about the way the old house was going to be the answer to everyone's prayers – everyone except Cat, that is.

"The only problem is that there's nothing left of it," grumbled Bean, kicking a stone, her eyes cast downwards as though an Elizabethan house would suddenly appear from under her boots.

"So how does that work, then?" Cat asked, not unreasonably. As I told you before, she was still a bit miffed with James and so wasn't going to get too excited by any ideas he came up with.

"It could be a site of historical interest," James explained, talking unnecessarily slowly as though Cat was being dim. You can imagine how well that went down with Cat.

"Historical interest to whom?" asked Cat.

"The. Nation. Of. Course," James said, even more slowly, just to annoy Cat. It worked.

"How. Is. The. Nation. Going. To. Know. About. It?" Cat replied, pouting at James.

"National Heritage!" said Katy. "They'll love it. They save old buildings for the nation. My mum's always dragging me around them in the school holidays. Some of them look as though they'd have been happier left to rot. Some are OK though, and quite interesting," she added.

"We'll get Sophie to tell them," added Bean. "She'll get them down here."

"Do you think Mrs Collins would mind?" I asked.

James dismissed my doubts. "Mind?" he said. "We're saving the stables, of course she won't mind."

We all whizzed back to the yard and found Sophie, told her breathlessly of our plans and left it in her hands. She was all for it, once we'd assured her that the house really had existed, according to Mrs Collins.

"Absolutely wonderful!" she gushed, pulling out her mobile. "I'll see who at National Heritage I can track down right now. Leave it with me."

So we did.

"That's sorted!" declared James, smugly.

"Yup!" agreed Katy. "You've saved us all, James. National Heritage will fall over itself to slap some sort of preservation order on the place, the development plans will grind to a halt and the ponies will all be able to stay here."

I thought about my Hickstead sash sacrifice. Could it be that Epona was helping us after all? Could it be that my sacrifice hadn't been in vain, but had done the trick?"

"Except for Bambi," Cat reminded her.

My heart sank and my thoughts returned to

Drummer and my beautiful Hickstead rosettes hanging on my bedroom wall. Would they have to join my sash in the flames before we could come up with a plan to save Bambi?

Chapter Seven

As if to rub it in how time for Bambi was running out, Cat's Aunt Pam brought her eldest daughter Emily to the yard at the weekend for a ride. And to emphasise how Bambi would soon no longer be Cat's responsibility, Aunt P took over as soon as Cat had tacked up her skewbald mare and led her out into the yard.

"Thanks," said her Aunt Pam, taking the reins from Cat and pulling them over Bambi's head, "I'll take it from here."

"Don't you want me to help you?" asked Cat, her face like stone.

"I can remember how to handle my own pony, thank you, Catriona!" her Aunt Pam said, testily, leading Bambi towards the outdoor school. Emily clutched her mother's free hand nervously, keeping a wary eye on her new pony, who neighed to Drummer as she left the yard. Pushing past me, Drum leaned on his stable door and neighed back, unhappy that his treasured Bambi was being repossessed, if only for an hour. In despair, Cat fled to the barn.

Bean gazed out from Tiffany's stable across the yard and we looked at each other helplessly.

"Come on," yelled Bean, closing Tiff's stable door behind her and making for the school, "let's see if we can get some inspiration from watching the enemy at work."

"Hurry up and do something!" Drummer pleaded with me as I locked his door and threw his dandy brush down on the ground outside his stable before following Bean. We couldn't very well stand and stare so we walked past the school as though we were going to the field, then doubled back and hid behind the jump store. As it was old and rickety, and the walls had gaping holes between the planks, it was quite easy to spy on Bambi. Emily was lifted bodily on to her broad back, and Aunt Pam adjusted her daughter's stirrups.

"Emily's too tiny to ride Bambi," hissed Bean. "Bambi's much too wide for her. She's practically doing the splits."

The child clutched the reins nervously, holding them

too short and too tightly. Bambi, unused to such treatment, put her head down and stretched her neck to get comfortable again, pulling the reins out of Emily's hands.

Emily screamed.

Screaming is never a good thing to do around ponies – as you know.

"If she was on Tiffany," Bean gasped, "she'd be in the next county by now."

Luckily, Bambi was no Tiffany. She just lifted her head warily, her ears back.

Aunt Pam told Emily off, adjusted her daughter's hands and started leading her around the school while Emily sat as stiff as a board, waggling the reins.

"Emily doesn't look as though she's ready for a pony of her own," I whispered.

"Mmmm," agreed Bean. "She'd probably be better off going for lessons at a riding school for a while, to give her some confidence."

"I suppose her mum can teach her," I said.

Emily's mum, it seemed, wasn't up for teaching. Whenever I'd seen Cat with Emily, she had shown her young cousin what to do and Emily had been a lot happier. Her mum, however, didn't look as though she could be bothered – she seemed to think Emily ought to know instinctively what to do in the saddle.

"Don't lean forward, Em," she grumbled. "Don't hold the reins so tightly. Don't dig your heels in like that."

Emily didn't take much notice. If anything, she held the reins tighter and dug her heels in to Bambi's sides even more.

"Wouldn't it be better if Aunt P told Emily what to do, instead of what not to?" I said. "She's not telling Emily what she should be doing, just what she shouldn't."

Bean nodded miserably.

"Can you stop pulling on the reins, please?" I heard Bambi say, screwing up her mouth. "And if you could get your heels out of my sides, I'd be grateful."

"Bambi's not impressed," I told Bean.

The trio continued around the school – and no-one looked especially happy. Then Aunt P decided it was time to go for a trot.

"Hold the saddle with one hand, Em, until you get going," she instructed as Bambi launched herself into her bouncy pace. Emily rattled around in the saddle, totally missing her bounce and getting only one rise to the trot in every six strides. It must have been very uncomfortable for her. She'd been OK with Cat helping her. I'd seen her trotting along, laughing with glee with Cat.

I had never appreciated before how patient Cat had been with her younger cousin, but now I could see that with Cat, Emily was far more confident and enjoyed riding Bambi. Now, that confidence had vanished. Aunt Pam seemed cross that her daughter didn't ride as well as she wanted her to. For everyone, including Bambi, it was a frustrating experience.

As Bambi was asked to walk again, Aunt Pam pushed Emily off Bambi's brown-and-white neck and back into the saddle.

"Phew," whispered Bean, "if Bambi was anything like Tiffany, Emily wouldn't even want to ride her, let alone have her at home with her. She'd be all over the place."

"I don't think I can watch any more," I said, and we both went back to the yard where James was in conversation with Sophie and Dee-Dee.

"Hey, you two," James called, beckoning us over, "Sophie has some news."

"A chap from National Heritage is coming over tomorrow to look at where the house was," Sophie told us, triumphantly.

"Yippee!" shouted Bean, punching the air. "That

was fast work!"

"Don't get too excited!" Sophie warned us. "It's just a preliminary visit to take a look and see what's around. There are no promises but the fact that he's interested is pretty encouraging."

"Will he have to meet Robert Collins?" asked James, frowning.

"Er, well, I sort of didn't tell him that I wasn't actually the owner of the land," Sophie said, ruefully. "He just seemed to assume that I had the authority, so I let him carry on thinking that. When things progress I'll get Mrs Collins involved."

"She lied," said Dee, pulling a face.

"No Dee, it isn't technically lying. I just . . . well . . . neglected to tell him the full facts at the moment."

"She lied," Dee mouthed to us behind her mum's back, her eyes wide and her mouth open in mock horror.

"Desperate measures for desperate times," said James, nodding.

"What happens when he finds out?" I asked.

"We'll cross that bridge when we come to it," Sophie replied, firmly. "First things first. We need to get some interest going, don't we? If the site is important, it won't matter who owns it, National Heritage will just refuse to let *anyone* build on it."

The sound of hoof beats heralded Bambi's return to the yard. Emily was once more walking beside her mother and Bambi's stirrups were run up their leathers, her girth slack.

As Cat came out to take Bambi from her aunt, we heard Aunt Pam say, "I think I'd better bring Emily up for some more rides on Bam-Bam before she comes back home, Cat. We'll say the first week in August, instead."

Cat just nodded, dumbly, not trusting herself to speak. I knew she hated the way her aunt called Bambi 'Bam-Bam'. Just calling her that seemed to highlight how Bambi belonged to her, not Cat.

We all watched Aunt Pam drive off with mixed feelings. Things were moving on. Mr National Heritage was booked to Save Our Stables on Tuesday evening and Bambi had a stay of execution, so to speak. We had another two weeks to come up with a plan for our Keep Bambi Campaign.

Would two weeks be enough?

Chapter Eight

You know how you always get a picture in your mind of how people are going to be? I had imagined the National Heritage man as pretty old, with grey hair and a matching moustache, wearing faded green tweed and with the air of an old army colonel. You know, all blustery and saying things like, "Well now!" and, "Look sharp!" and the like. And because he was from National Heritage, I somehow assumed he'd drive a very old, rather expensive car.

How wrong was I?

The man who got out of the small, modern, rather boring grey car couldn't have looked less like an army type. He looked like a student. A bearded, long-haired, khaki-wearing student. Looking around the yard, he reached into one of his pockets and pulled out a packet of cigarettes and a box of matches.

"You can't smoke in a stable yard!" Katy yelled at him from Bluey's stable.

The man dropped his unlit cigarette in alarm and gazed intently at Bluey, probably thinking he'd come to a stable full of talking horses. Which he had, only without Epona, there was no way *he* was going to hear them.

Seeing me in the tackroom, the NH man raised his hand in greeting and told me he had an appointment with Mrs Wiseman.

"I'll get her," I told him, running around the corner and yelling for Sophie. Then Katy and I shamelessly eavesdropped.

"You believe you have an Elizabethan structure here?" the man asked.

"Oh yes," Sophie assured him, switching off her mobile. Things were that serious!

"Very exciting, very exciting," breathed the NH man. "Not many of them around, we need all the ones we can get, frankly."

"Yes," Sophie replied, "I was hoping you'd say that."

Katy and I exchanged glances. It sounded promising.

"Too many of these wonderful old places are lost," Mr NH Man continued, searching his pockets for his cigarettes. Then, remembering Katy's scolding, he returned them to a different pocket, running his fingers through his hair instead.

"Well, let me show you," Sophie said, and they both walked out to the field. Katy and I followed at a distance and leant on the gate, waving to Dee who was schooling Dolly in the outdoor school. Sophie had instructed her daughter to work on her transitions, apparently they'd been shaky at her last show, and Dee was thrilled. Not.

"This is totally going to work," Katy said, her elbows on the gate, chin in her hands.

I sighed. It had to, really.

A few minutes passed. We watched Henry the black Dales pony scratch his rear end on the trunk of the old oak tree. Pippin, the smallest pony on the yard, walked over to the water trough for a drink, droplets of water dripping from his lips as he lifted his head and stared at something in the distance that we couldn't see, and I could see Drummer standing very still, right at the far end of the field. He was probably trying to make out he wasn't there so I wouldn't bring him in and go riding.

"Look out, they're coming back," I said, as Sophie and the NH man returned at a brisk walk. We skidaddled into the barn, feeling like a couple of (not very good) spies. As the gate clicked shut, we could hear their conversation.

"I do feel you have got me here under false pretences." (NH man)

"Absolutely not!" (Sophie)

"I was led to believe the structure was still standing, that there was something to save for the nation." (NH man)

"I thought you people were interested in historical sites." (Sophie)

"There's nothing to see!" (NH man)

Sophie didn't seem to have an answer to this – which was a first as far as I could remember.

Katy and I looked at one another in horror. It was obvious that National Heritage couldn't give a hoot about our Elizabethan house. Or, more correctly, where our Elizabethan house had been.

"He doesn't care!" said Katy, indignantly.

My heart sank into my boots. What were we going to do now? Making our way round to the yard we were just in time to see the back of Mr NH man's grey car disappear down the drive, back to where he came from, unimpressed by our historical site.

Sophie was down but not out.

"He's only interested in actual buildings," she told

us, tapping her toe on the concrete as she went into full re-think mode.

"But that means we're sunk!" I cried, unable to quite believe it. When the day had begun, the stables were saved. Now, it seemed, all was doomed. And we still hadn't got a plan for our Keep Bambi Campaign, my memory reminded me, annoyingly! AND I'd sacrificed my Hickstead sash for diddly squat! I felt my heart dip and I really thought a tear or two was getting ready to drizzle out of my eyes. I'd had such high hopes of National Heritage.

"Only for the time being," muttered Sophie, still thinking. "Keep at it girls, there has to be a way to get round this," she told us as she marched off to continue doing whatever it was she'd been doing before Mr NH-time-waster-man had interrupted her.

Katy and I sat on a straw bale outside Tiffany's stable and I pulled myself together. What a blow! Neither of us said anything, there were no words. We were both struck a bit dumb by the turn of events. From being up there, all positive, we were suddenly plunged once more into despair. I felt a bit sick. I could still hear the sizzling sound my sash had made when it had gone up in flames.

"What a bummer!" Katy said at last, ripping bits of

straw out of Bean's bale in frustration and throwing them to the ground.

Bluey stuck his head over his door and asked us what was up.

"The National Heritage people aren't interested in the site," I explained. "They only want proper buildings. Our building is no more."

"I know, I was there," sighed Katy.

"I'm explaining to Bluey," I explained to his owner.

"Oh," said Bluey. Then, not able to think up any words of comfort, or possibly wanting to return to nosing around his bed, he withdrew again.

"Where is everyone?" asked Katy. It was almost five o'clock and everyone else was usually at the yard after school by now. As if she'd heard her, Bean pedalled down the drive and threw herself off her bike.

"Has he been?" she asked. "Are we saved?"

"Yes, he's been," I told her.

"No, we're not saved," Katy spat out. "Mr National-poxy-Heritage wasn't impressed. He expected a huge building with turrets and stuff, like Hampton Court."

"Is Hampton Court Elizabethan?" I asked. "I thought it was built before that."

"I thought castles had turrets," mumbled Bean. "So does that mean we've failed?"

77

"It looks like it," I groaned, trying once again not to think about my sash. I mean, in the great scheme of things a sash was nothing to worry about, was it?

"Where is everyone?" asked Bean, looking around.

I shrugged my shoulders. "Cat's not here and there's no James yet, and he said he was coming riding with us. Dee's schooling Dolly in the outdoor school. Are you going to get Tiffany in? I'll come with you and get Drummer."

Bean put her hands on her hips and stared at us both. "Is that my straw bale you're demolishing?" she asked, frowning.

We left Katy quietly fuming in the yard as we made our way out into the field to catch the ponies. Drummer was still at the far end so I had a long walk to get him. He wasn't very impressed at having to leave Bambi, but there was no way she was going to come in with him if she didn't have to.

"Was that the historical bloke I saw out here?" Drum asked me as I led him towards the gate after Tiffany's white tail.

I nodded. "He's not interested. Only wants proper buildings or ruins. He was very dismissive of the possibility of a site without any actual bricks and mortar."

"Oh," said Drummer. "What are we going to do now?"

78

"We don't know."

"Oh."

We reached the gate. Went through it.

"What's your contingency plan?" Drum asked.

"Haven't got one," I told him, fastening the gate behind us.

"Oh."

"Can't you say anything else but *oh*?"

"Yes, but you wouldn't want to hear it!"

Katy, Bean and I all went for a ride, hoping to lift our spirits. It didn't work. I just kept wondering how much longer we'd be able to ride on the bridlepaths, how many more times we'd enjoy a gallop on the Sloping Field, or a charge through the Winding Canter. The mood was sombre, whereas before we had been optimistic. Even Tiffany seemed down, and shied less than usual.

When we got back, James had arrived – and Cat's brother Dec was with him. He'd been coming to the yard now and again with James since he'd helped out on our activity ride at Christmas. Everyone knew why. Declan has the hots for Bean. Good looking, despite his hair nowadays being a sort of rust-and-blonde colour, he always wears clothes that could have fitted another person in with him. As usual, he kept staring at Bean in adoration. I don't know how she manages to ignore him, especially as she's aware of his crush.

"Where have you been, James?" demanded Katy. "It's almost seven o'clock. I thought you were coming riding with us."

"Change of plan," James told her, grinning.

"How come?" I asked.

"Bit of a problem at school."

"Such as?" asked Bean.

"Oh, nothing," James answered, airily.

"Not much!" interrupted Dec, grinning shyly at Bean. "He got three detentions today."

"Three!" exclaimed Katy, who never gets detentions. "That's going some, James, even for you. Whatever did you do?"

"Mistaken identity!" James said, winking at me in a conspiratorial sort of way. My heart did a flip. I wish I could control it but I can't. I've given up trying to.

"What, all three times?" Bean asked. "Come off it!"

"I've done my time and paid my dues and I'm ready to move on," James said dramatically. "What news from the front, anyway?"

"Has National Heritage saved the day?" Dec asked, obviously fully briefed by his friend as well as his sister.

We told them both the sorry story. The mood got even glummer – especially when Dee joined us.

"This SOOOOOO sucks!" she wailed, throwing her hat in her tackbox so hard it rebounded out again and bounced along the floor, coming to rest under the tap, which dripped into it.

"You know you're not supposed to wear a hat that's been bashed, don't you?" Katy told her. "It's probably damaged and you'll need a new one."

"Oh it's all right," Dee told her, picking it up and brushing it off. "I'm always dropping it."

"No, Katy's right . . ." began Bean.

"Never mind Dee's hat," cried James, "our only hope of saving Laurel Farm has failed. What are we going to do?"

"We'd better start looking for new homes for the ponies," said Dee, utterly defeated.

"Don't say that!" yelled Katy, her eyes blazing.

"We don't have much choice," Dee wailed.

Suddenly, Cat arrived in her mum's car, slamming the door shut and running over to where we were all stood in a dejected crowd outside the tackroom. He eyes were blazing and her cheeks flushed and as she came to an abrupt halt she ran her fingers through her short, dark hair so that it stood up in spikes on top of her head. She managed to look both furious and despairing at once.

"Have you seen what's been nailed to the telegraph pole by the entrance to the yard?" she yelled.

I didn't much care. I didn't think anything could make this day any worse.

I was wrong. Again.

"There's a notice to say that horrible Robert Collins has applied for planning permission for twelve dwellings on the site of Laurel Farm. It's going to go through, I know it is, and we'll never be able to stop it!"

The vision of my Hickstead sash, burning and smoking in our fire at home, swam before my eyes. My sacrifice had definitely been in vain.

Chapter Nine

"Twelve dwellings!" James read out, standing on tiptoe as the notice had been put quite high up on the telegraph pole.

"Told you!" snapped Cat, furiously.

"I thought someone said there were going to be *hundreds* of houses?" I asked.

"Twelve – hundreds, what's the difference?" Katy replied, shrugging her shoulders.

The vision of a huge housing estate melted in my mind, replaced by a few sorry-looking houses scattered about.

"It says here . . . er . . . basically, it says that anyone with any objection should let the council know," James said, reading from the plastic-covered notice.

"Why don't we just rip it down and burn it?" I suggested.

"Because someone else might have some objections and that could help our case," said Katy. "If they can't read it, they can't object."

"Who is there to object? There's no-one else within miles!" Bean pointed out.

"That's true, we're the only ones who are going to be affected," James agreed.

"Well, let's object then!" I said. It seemed so obvious.

"No one will care about ponies having to move out. They mean people," Dee said. "*People* have to object."

The notice fluttered in the breeze. It was like a death sentence, I thought, looking at it. A black-and-white notice of misery.

"I suppose some people would welcome it," Katy said, almost to herself. "I mean, look at the view – imagine having a house here. I expect a lot of people would be interested in buying a house in this area."

"Like the Elizabethans," Bean said, quietly.

"Well, they haven't helped," Katy replied. "If they'd built their house a bit better it might still be here and we might feel a lot differently right now."

"They'll all be big, expensive houses," said James, still reading. We all looked at the board under the notice which had a picture of a new house and a laughing couple in a dining room. "LAUREL

HEIGHTS . . ." it said in big letters.

"What's *Laurel Heights*?" I asked.

"The development," explained Cat, still seething.

"That's what he's calling it, apparently," James explained, reading aloud from the smaller letters underneath. "*Laurel Heights, a select, contemporary development in tranquil surroundings – get tomorrow's lifestyle, today.*"

"You can't get it today," Bean pointed out. "It's not built yet."

James continued reading from the notice. "It says here permission is sought for nine five-bedroom houses, two eight-bedroom houses and a barn conversion. I mean, they're not going to be cheap, are they? It's hardly affordable housing our chum Robert is planning. It's not as though he's providing for people without homes. Has anyone got a pen?"

"Barn conversion?" echoed Katy.

"What a cheek!" exploded Cat. "He's going to turn our barn into some horrible house. What do you want a pen for, James?"

"What? Our lovely barn where we keep the ponies' feed and hay?" whispered Bean.

"Your part of it isn't lovely," Katy told her, miserably. "It's a right mess. Here's a pen."

Bean pulled a face. Like that was important. James took Katy's pen and started drawing moustaches on the laughing couple on the board.

"Oh that's mature!" Katy said.

"It makes me feel better," James told her.

"They'd look better if the ink was black instead of blue," Cat pointed out.

"Details, details!" James replied, adding some geeky round specs.

My imaginary estate of twelve sorry-looking houses turned into a plush development of huge mansions, front doors flanked by snowy-white columns and spherical trees in metal containers along the drives.

After James had added beards and a few spots to the laughing couple, we dawdled back along the drive to the yard. Still angry, Cat was looking for someone to kick. She picked her brother.

"What are you doing here?" she asked him, poking his arm with her finger.

"He's with me," James told her.

"I'm asking Dec, not you," Cat replied.

"Oh, let's not argue!" exploded Katy. "We need to stay united if we're ever going to stop Robert Collins's plans and another brain isn't something to turn down."

"Brain? That's a laugh!" Cat snorted.

"Talking of plans," Dec said, "how are the ones for the Keep Bambi Campaign coming along?"

Everyone groaned.

"Not so good, I take it," Dec said, throwing his sister an exaggerated smile. He'd successfully got her back where it hurt.

We all did what we had to do – it was too late to ride. Cat ran out to check on Bambi, James and Dec followed in the same direction at a distance, to see Moth. Katy and Bean turned out Bluey and Tiffany and Dee had orders from her mum to change Lester and Dolly's water and give them haynets. They were both still stabled – the show season had started so their diets had to be carefully controlled, not to mention their exercise. Once the grass had gone off a bit, Sophie would turn them out at night like the other ponies. It was the start of what Dee described, rather over-dramatically, as her dark season. Her time was not her own and she wasn't allowed to do anything with Dolly without her mum's say-so.

With a sigh, I brushed Drum's saddle mark out of his back and sponged his eyes and nose, explaining about the notice.

"Things are going from bad to worse," he snorted.

"Yes," I said, unable to think of anything else.

"Perhaps you're all trying too hard."

"What do you mean? How can we try too hard?"

"Oh, well, sometimes the best solutions to problems just sort of occur when you're not consciously thinking of them," Drummer told me.

That didn't make sense but I couldn't be bothered to argue with Drummer. I felt limp, like a piece of chewed string.

I put Drum's headcollar on him and led him out to the field. Dolly stretched her nose out to him as we walked past her stable.

"I wish I was coming out with you, Drummer," she sighed.

"Yeah, well, it won't be long," he told her.

As soon as Drummer had gobbled up the apple I'd brought him he dashed off to see Bambi, only rolling once he was with her. Cat was back in the yard but I could see James and Dec on the far side of the field under a tree with Moth. James was checking Moth over and Dec was hanging by his arms from one of the tree's branches like an overdressed gibbon.

The sun hung like a huge, red ball in the sky which was turning pink. It was going to be a glorious sunset – but I wouldn't see it before I went home, there was still ages left before the sun went down.

I could imagine how popular houses on this site would be – who wouldn't want to live with that view?

James and Dec made their way back to the gate and we all walked into the yard together. Everyone was still there. Everyone was still gloomy.

"Phew!" puffed Katy, delving into her tackbox for a can of Coke which she opened with a *pssst!* "It's still hot, isn't it?" she continued brightly, determined to lighten the mood.

No-one else wanted to.

"I can't believe we're going to have to leave here," mumbled Dee.

"Do you think we'll all be able to move to another yard together?" asked Bean.

"Not likely!" said James. "What livery yard is going to have six places going begging all at once?"

"Where's Lester going?" asked Dee. "You've missed him out."

"And Henry, and Pippin and Mr Higgins," said Katy.

"Leanne isn't bothered – she'll go to some dressage yard," James told her.

"You're forgetting something," said Cat, glumly, "Bambi's already got a new home so Lester can have her place."

Everyone went quiet.

"We watched Emily riding Bambi the other day," Bean said, staring into space.

"Did you?" asked Cat. "What, while I was in the yard? I didn't know."

"We thought it might provide some inspiration," I explained.

"It didn't," added Bean.

"How did Emily get on?" asked Cat, curious despite herself.

"Bambi's too much for Emily right now," I said, remembering the child's frightened face as she'd ridden around the school.

"But she'll get better," Katy replied. "It's not like Bambi is like Tiffany, all dodging about and getting hysterical at the sight of a crisp bag, or an oversized worm. Emily will soon be as confident as anything."

"Yeah, if I'd got Tiffany before I was a half-decent rider, she'd have put me off riding for life," Bean laughed. "I'd never have wanted a pony – at least, not one like Tiffany!"

Everyone was silent. Everyone, except for Bean, was thinking the same thing. You could almost hear the whirring of collective brains in the evening air.

"That's it!" cried James.

"Of course!"

"Sorted!"

"Why didn't we think of it before?"

"That's genius, Bean!" (That was Dec – of course.)

"Oh, that is so going to work!"

"What is?" asked Bean, confused.

Leaping up, Cat threw her arms around Bean and gave her a hug. "I do believe you have just come up with the most delicious plan!" she told her.

"I have?"

"Somebody explain it to her," said James, shaking his head.

"Bambi will need to make like Tiffany for a while," I told her.

Bean frowned in confusion.

"Just enough to prove to Aunt Pam that she isn't a suitable mount for Emily," continued Dec.

"But only enough to scare her a bit," Katy said, doubtfully. "It would be horrible if we scared her so much she gave up riding altogether."

"Oh yes, of course," agreed Cat, quickly, almost managing to convince herself if no one else.

"How will Bambi know what to do?" Bean asked.

Four pairs of eyes swung my way. I grinned.

"Ahhhh, of course!" sighed Bean. "Well, who'd have

thought I'd be the one to come up with a plan for our Keep Bambi Campaign?"

"Not me, for a start," James mumbled.

"Shame you didn't realise you'd hit on it!" Cat told her.

"And we'll need Pia to brief Bambi and put the plan into action," Katy pointed out.

"That's teamwork for you!" said Dec.

"I've got to tell Drummer!" I said, running towards the field. He was going to be so relieved we'd come up with a plan – when we hadn't been trying, just like he'd said. How did he do that?

"And Bambi!" Cat called after me. "Tell Bambi, too!"

Chapter Ten

"OK!" Katy said briskly, rubbing her hands together. "Let's recap on what we have got and what we haven't."

"I *have* got to clean my tack," grumbled Dee.

"And we *haven't*!" giggled Bean.

"You can help me, then," Dee told her, flinging a wet sponge across the yard. It landed, splat, on Bean's knee, leaving her with a wet patch on her pink, chequered jodhpurs.

"That's soaking, and cold!" she squealed.

"That's good, coming from someone who washes their hair in the yard," James said.

"I meant plan-wise," Katy reminded us.

"We *have* got a plan for the Keep Bambi Campaign," said Cat, punching the air.

"We *haven't* been so lucky with our Stables SOS," James said, sighing. "So even if we are successful

93

and Bambi stays, we may all still come up one day to find our ponies tied to the fence with their suitcases packed."

"Tiffany hasn't got a suitcase," said Bean, puzzled. James threw her a look of despair. "Oh, I get it," said Bean, matching James's glare. "Very funny!"

"Not really," mumbled Cat.

Katy stroked Cat's arm reassuringly. "We're not beaten yet, are we?"

"No!" everyone chorused. I wondered whether they felt the same as me – although I joined in with a resounding NO with everyone else, I felt far from confident that we would ever be able to save the stables.

"We just need another idea," said Bean. "A second chance."

"Exactly! And of course we're doing this for Mrs Collins, too," Katy reminded us. "I bet she doesn't want to go into some home. She'll miss her cats and Squish."

"I wouldn't miss that Twiddles-scissor-paws," Dee said, looking around in case he materialised out of thin air. "He's a monster cat."

"Not with Mrs C, he isn't," I reminded her.

A car trundled down the drive. Nobody recognised

it and we all looked up, wondering who it could be.

It was the enemy, Robert Collins.

Stopping the car outside his mother's house, he got out and unlocked the front door, closing it behind him as he disappeared inside.

"What do you think he's up to?" I asked.

"Do you think he's come to get her stuff?" Katy said. "Do you think Mrs C is off to the home?"

"She might be dead," suggested James.

"Oh James!" exclaimed Bean. "That is so horrid! You don't think she really is, do you?"

"My mum said she was looking much better when she went to see her last night, so I doubt it," Dee told us, glaring at James.

"What else did she say?" Cat asked Dee.

"Nothing much. Mrs C doesn't seem to have any notion of her son's plans to bung her in a home. She kept telling Mum about her idea for her stair lift and asking after the cats."

"She really has no idea?" I asked.

"That is so cruel," Bean whispered.

The door to the house flew open again and Robert Collins came out clutching some papers. He seemed to notice us for the first time and waved half-heartedly with a weak smile.

Nobody waved back. It would have been like waving to William the Conqueror in 1066. You know: *Come on in, Bill me old mate, suppress us, give our land to your lords and tax us till we bleed and we'll give you a winning smile, you cheeky little monkey, you!* Maybe not quite as bad as that, but you get the general idea.

Robert Collins jumped in his car, did a three-point turn on the gravel and sped off up the drive in a cloud of dust.

"Do you reckon they're the deeds to the place he's got there?" Cat asked, gravely.

"Who knows?" said James.

That was the worst of it, I thought. It was horrible, not knowing exactly what Robert Collins was up to.

That evening, when I got home, I sat on my bed looking first at Epona sitting on my dressing table, and then at my beautiful Hickstead rosettes. I couldn't help wondering whether I really would have to make another sacrifice. Was it coincidence that we'd come up with a plan for our Keep Bambi Campaign the day after I had thrown my beautiful sash in the fire? Standing on my bed I lifted my beautiful first and second place Hickstead rosettes down from the wall, together with the orange and lime Sublime

Equine rosette. OK, so they were a bit dusty, but they were still gorgeous.

Something fluttered down to the floor. A small, rectangular piece of white card. Jumping off the bed I bent down, flipping it up with my thumbnail, and was about to throw it in the bin when I noticed it had writing on the other side.

Alex Willard, Equine Behaviourist, I read. His address and telephone number were underneath in smaller writing. Under that was www.alexwillard.com. He'd given it to me when we'd both been on an afternoon TV show and I suddenly remembered why I had hidden it there. My mum, tipsy with wine and – there was no other word for it – desperate, had mistakenly believed that Alex Willard fancied her and had threatened to call him. How embarrassing would that have been? Behind my Hickstead rosette had seemed a good place to hide the card. I didn't want my mum to find it and be tempted.

We had seen him again at the Riding for the Disabled Equine Extravaganza at Christmas. That time, I remembered, Alex *had* fancied my mum because she had been smiley and happy and very different – because she had been with Mike. She was still with Mike. She was still smiley and happy, I thought.

Alex Willard . . . He was a *name*. He was a *celebrity* – even non-horsey people had heard of Alex Willard. He'd been on TV loads of times. I wondered . . .

Switching on my computer I waited impatiently for the screen to flicker into life. I was no stranger to Alex Willard's website – it was at the very top of my list of favourites. I often went on it to look at his case studies and tried to soak up some of his techniques – although since I could talk to Drum, I hadn't been on it so much. Things were a bit easier if you could actually communicate with horses.

Alex wouldn't have given me his card if he hadn't been OK about me contacting him, I thought. If I had needed any help with Drummer or anything, that's why he'd handed it over.

Well, I needed help now. Big time.

I clicked on Contact Alex and an email page came up.

What could I say?

What made me think he could help?

What did I think he could do?

How on earth could he do anything?

It's only an email, I thought, and started typing.

Chapter Eleven

The next time Cat's Aunt Pam brought Emily to see her darling Bam-Bam, our Keep Bambi Campaign had been initiated. Darling Bam-Bam was fully primed, ready to go and anything but darling!

"I wouldn't like to do anything that will hurt Emily," Bambi had said to me after I'd outlined what she had to do to put Cat's cousin off wanting Bambi to be her own pony.

"No, we wouldn't like that, either," I'd agreed, nodding furiously. Drummer had been with us – we were out in the field after school under one of the trees, and Cat, Katy, James and Bean had all been there, too.

"Tell her she just has to be a little bit too lively for a beginner," Cat had interrupted. She'd kept butting in. I suppose I would have done, too, if she'd been able to understand equine instead of me. I didn't want to think about that. If Cat had found Epona instead of me, that was exactly what would be happening. Not a nice thought, even if we were actually on civilised speaking terms these days.

"Look," I had explained to Bambi, "you just need to pretend you're not as nice as you really are. You know how you're always putting your ears back and lunging at people over your stable door, giving them the heebie-jeebies? You just need to exaggerate that a bit."

Bambi was always pulling faces and pretending to be fierce, but she was only bluffing. Now it was time to make it for real.

"You know how you behaved with me when I first arrived here?" Drummer had chimed in. "You were a bit of a misery guts, weren't you?"

"Misery guts?" Bambi had repeated, drawing herself up and giving Drum a filthy look. "Misery guts?!"

"Yeah, that's right, just like you're doing now. That's perfect!" Drum had told her, wading right on in.

"You thought I was a *misery guts*?" Bambi had continued, unwilling to let it lie.

Ooops.

"What's Bambi saying?" Cat had asked.

"Come on Pia, keep us up-to-date!" James had insisted.

"I think she knows what she has to do," I had told them, and we'd gone back to the yard leaving Bambi and Drum in a full-scale argument behind us. I could hear all kinds of equine insults being hurled back and forth. At this rate, I'd thought, Drum would be glad to see the back of Bambi and wave her off the yard. But the next day they were all lovey-dovey again, having made up. Honestly, they were worse than my mum and Mike-the-bike when they were like that.

And today, Aunt Pam and Emily were back and we were all anxious to see whether Bambi could pull off her horrid-pony-act. Not too much, not too little. It was going to be a tough balancing act. I think everyone was on tenterhooks.

As Cat led Bambi out of her stable, Bean, Katy and I huddled together in Tiffany's empty stable, watching out of her window.

I say watching . . .

"Crikey, Bean," hissed Katy, "you might as well not bother with a window in this stable, it's so full of grime and cobwebs."

Bean just shrugged her shoulders.

"We should have gone in my stable," Katy grumbled, "at least you can see through Bluey's window."

"Shhhh," I told her, peering through the gloom.

101

"Who cares about the window?" Bambi clamped her ears back along her neck and snaked her head up and down as Emily went towards her. Emily retreated behind her mother.

Poor Emily, I thought, my conscience bothering me.

"Well done, Bambi!" Katy whispered, ruthlessly.

"I thought you said you couldn't see anything!" Bean whispered, miffed.

I looked across to Moth's stable, opposite, where James and Dee were hiding and spying out of Moth's window. All the ponies were in the field, although I knew Drummer would be at the gate, waiting for Bambi to be turned out again when Aunt Pam and Emily had gone.

Aunt Pam took Bambi from Cat and made for the school again, with Emily trailing along beside her. Bambi jogged a bit, making like a hyped-up Derby favourite in the parade ring, her quarters swinging from side to side as she arched her neck and snorted.

"Whatever is up with you, Bam-Bam?" we heard Aunt Pam ask her. As soon as the trio were out of site, we all had a pow-wow in the yard.

"Do you really think this will work?" asked Cat, biting her nails.

"Yeah, of course!" James said, breezily.

Bean narrowed her eyes and clapped her hands. "Let's go and watch," she said, with all the gory enthusiasm of a citizen of Ancient Rome off to watch gladiators in the Colosseum.

"Oooh yes!" Dee agreed, and we cautiously made our way around the corner to watch from the barn.

Obviously I was the only one to feel for Emily.

"I can't watch," Cat told us, turning around and going back to the yard. "It's too painful."

We could only see half of the school from there, but Drummer could see all of it from the field gate, and I heard him shouting encouragement to Bambi.

"Why don't you put in a bit of a buck there?" I heard him cry, followed by an Emily-sounding squeal as Bambi put his suggestion into practice. Bambi's brown-and-white form came into view at the C end and we saw Aunt Pam holding Emily's left leg as Bambi danced about a bit on the end of her lead rein. Not too much, just enough to make it uncomfortable. There was really never any chance of Emily falling off, but it certainly couldn't have been at all enjoyable.

Suddenly, Cat was at our side.

"I thought it was too painful to watch?" asked Katy.

"More painful not to," Cat explained, pulling a face.

Another circuit, more suggestions from Drummer,

more squeaking from Emily.

"I hope she's not overdoing it," Cat muttered, still chewing her nails. At least she seemed to have some sympathy for her small cousin.

"I'm sure she isn't," Katy assured her, soothingly.

"Emily sounds well spooked," said James.

"Poor Emily," Bean sympathised, softening. "I hope we don't put her off riding all together."

Bambi came back into view. Aunt Pam was riding her.

"Uh-oh," said James.

Cat groaned. "She's going to tell Bambi off, isn't she?" she said.

But Bambi, egged on by Drummer, was giving Aunt Pam a much harder time than she had Emily, and was plunging, shaking her head and lifting her back end in miniature bucks, all the time squealing and snorting.

"Go Bambi!" encouraged Drummer.

"She sounds like a dragon!" Dee giggled.

"Brilliant Bambi!" Katy agreed.

"Aunt P can't possibly want to have her back now," said James.

The pair disappeared from view again and we all looked at each other. Our plan seemed to be going stonkingly well. Bambi was being bad, but not mad or dangerous and even Aunt Pam wasn't getting an easy ride. Surely she'd think twice about having her darling Bam-Bam back at home at this rate.

After ten minutes or so, we heard the gate to the school open.

"Quick Cat, get back to the yard!" Dee said, giving Cat a shove. Cat sped off back to Bambi's stable to offer an innocent greeting to her returning relatives and we all huddled in the barn so we wouldn't be seen.

"That seemed to go well," James said, rubbing his hands together in satisfaction.

"I hope so," I said. "Bambi certainly got the idea."

"Yup, all sorted," Dee agreed. "I bet Aunt Pam will be only too happy to let Cat keep Bambi now that she's proved how unsuitable she is for young Emily."

"Shhhh!" hissed Katy, her finger to her lips. "Isn't that the sound of Aunt P's car going?"

We raced around to the yard and leaned over Bambi's half door to gawp at Cat and her pony.

"Well?" asked James.

"Wasn't Bambi brill?" said Bean.

"Yeah, well done Bambi!" I told her.

Bambi snorted. "Yeah, I think I did a pretty good job," she said, shaking her head.

"Has your Aunt Pam changed her mind, then?" asked Dee.

"Not exactly," Cat said, pulling a face.

"Why, what did she say?" I asked her. We'd gone all congratulatory too soon, it appeared.

"She said I needed to cut Bambi's feed and that she'd be back next week to ride her again," Cat said. "My Aunt Pam was not impressed. She said I'd let her darling Bam-Bam get bad habits and that she would have to – in her words – sort her out."

"What does that mean?" asked Bambi, her eyes wide.

"Don't worry," I said, soothingly.

"Don't worry!" exploded Cat. "Don't worry! How would you like it if she'd threatened to sort Drummer out?"

"I was talking to Bambi," I mumbled.

"I am worried!" Bambi said, looking very worried. "I don't like the sound of being sorted out. Let her sort you out!"

"Oh dear," said Katy, her mouth like an upside down banana.

"Whoops!" Dee added.

"Whoops! Whoops! Is that all you lot can come up with, *whoops*?" Bambi said, shaking her head, her ears flat against her mane. "Whose brilliant idea was this?"

I couldn't remember. I just knew it hadn't been mine. I told the others what Bambi had said.

"Sorry," mumbled Bean. "Only, in my defence, I hadn't actually realised I'd had the idea – someone else picked it up and ran with it."

"Who?" asked Bambi, looking around at everyone.

"Who?" I repeated because nobody could hear her but me.

No one owned up. Everyone looked in different directions, or at the floor, or suddenly found their finger nails riveting. No one was taking credit for that one – not any more. My heart sank as I realised Drummer would have something to say when Bambi gave him an update. And because I was the only one who could hear him, I was going to get it in the neck. I wondered how it would be if I left Epona at home for a few days.

Suddenly, another car came along the drive and pulled up outside Mrs Collins's house. We all made like nosy neighbours, turning to take a good look as the engine was turned off.

I know that car, I thought, frowning.

"Wow, fantastic car!" breathed James, as the doors opened and a man and a woman got out of the red sports number, slamming the doors shut again and waving at me.

"Who's that?" asked Cat.

"That," I replied, wondering just how much further my heart could sink before dropping out on to the yard, "is my dad and his girlfriend."

"Yoo-hoo Pia!" gurgled Skinny Lynny, her blonde hair tied up in a messy ponytail, her body poured into a skin-tight T-shirt and yellow cotton jeans. They both came over and gave me unnecessary hugs.

"Hi Pia, we thought we might see you here," said my dad.

Strange thing to say, I thought. Why else would they be here if not to see me? And that in itself was a bit odd. I mean, they don't make a habit of dropping in unannounced – thank goodness.

"Er, hi," I said, confused.

"We're here to look at a plot," said Skinny, crinkling her nose up as she gave me the benefit of her cutest smile. It might work on my dad but it cuts no ice with me. I just stared back at her.

"Plot?" I asked. As in lost it, I presumed.

"That's right," said my dad, nodding and looking around. "We saw the notice for the new houses here and we thought we'd take a look with a view to buying off-plan – you know, get in early and get a bargain price. Apparently the view is amazing!"

"It will be like living in the country!" giggled Skinny. "Come on Paul, let's go and take a look at where plot two will be – unless you've really got your heart set on the barn conversion, but I still think the view from plot two will be better. Bring the leaflet."

Icy fingers clutched at my heart and hauled it back up off the yard and into my mouth. They couldn't be serious! As the pair of them toddled off to lean over the gate and gaze out at the ponies' field, picturing a new idyllic life in the country with floral aprons and freshly baked bread I could feel everyone's eyes upon me.

"That's the end!" said Katy. "Don't tell me people are going to be coming up to view where they want their houses to be!"

"They're nothing to do with me!" I protested, wishing it were true.

"They're the people who are going to live in the barn!" wailed Bean. "The ones with a sports car in the car port where Drummer's stable is now!"

Anger bubbled up inside me. Not only did Skinny Lynny have my dad, but she now wanted our barn and Drummer's stable.

I wish I'd saved my sash to strangle her with.

Chapter Twelve

When I got home Mum and Mike were out. There was
no bike outside, so I assumed they'd gone on an
evening motorbike ride in the country somewhere,
which is what they're into. I've come to terms with
my mum wearing leather biker gear. Sort of. I suppose
it could be worse. I mean, Bean's family are all
into music and the arts, making a mess and a noise
all over the house. At least Mum and Mike disappear
on the bike, they don't ride it all around the sitting
room, getting in the way and preventing me from
hearing the TV.

What a day, I thought, doing my best to forget it.
First our Bambi plan not going – well, to plan – and
then Dad and Skinny Lynny showing up and talking
about buying one of the houses at Laurel Heights. Talk
about poo central. I couldn't see any way we could

possibly save the stables. Everything was happening despite our efforts.

I had chickened out of seeing Drummer again. I couldn't face his comments when Bambi told him about Aunt P's plans for her next week. I'd face that particular trial tomorrow. And besides, I remembered, I could always 'forget' to take Epona with me, even though that was just deferring Drum's wrath and being very, very cowardly. I felt a bit cowardly, to be honest. Everything was starting to get to me.

Going upstairs to my room, I switched on my computer out of habit, angrily throwing all my stables clothes in a heap on the floor, treading on my jodhpurs to get them off my legs. I felt I couldn't be bothered with anything any more.

The computer *dinked* and I glanced at the screen.

I had mail.

My email icon was blinking at me.

I'd emailed Alex Willard, I remembered, my heart doing a flip.

Was it a good blink or a disappointment blink, I thought? Scared to open it, I struggled into my jeans and a sweat shirt, staring at the icon, putting off the moment, my throat suddenly dry.

It might not even be from Alex, I thought. But what

if it was? Well, I thought, if it is from Alex he's already written it, so hesitating won't change what's inside. I could feel my heart thumping in my chest as I clicked the cursor on the icon and my email screen flipped open, revealing the email address to be Alex's. It's probably from his secretary, I thought, giving me a standard reply to my begging letter, "thanks but no thanks" . . .

It wasn't from Alex's secretary.

It was from Alex.

Dear Pia, I read, *Thank you for your email, it was lovely to hear from you. I was interested to learn about the site of an old house in your ponies' field and do have a contact at one of the TV companies who may be interested in getting a team of archaeologists to take a look. She produces the programme Time Detectives, which you may have seen (she also produced a programme I made about equine behaviour, which is how I know her!).*

In Time Detectives, a group of archaeologists examine and dig up remains at old sites, looking for historical artefacts and evidence of settlements in times gone by. Your old house sounds just the sort of thing they'd be interested in. I've taken the liberty of emailing her for you, and shall get back to you as soon as I hear from her. Her name's Jessica Tamarad.

I let out the breath I'd been holding. Could this really be happening? I glanced up at my Hickstead rosettes and decided I didn't need to chuck them into the sacrificial fire just yet.

I read on . . .

I hope you and your mother are well, Alex wrote, *and that I shall be able to get involved should Jessica take this further. I've always been interested in our history – don't you find it fascinating? How exciting to have the remains of an Elizabethan house in your field. It could be a very important find! If Jessica does want to film with Time Detectives, they will need to dig up the field – but if there is evidence of an important house on the site, they'll work with the authorities to make sure you are compensated. I know that Time Detectives works with National Heritage if the site is of historical importance, and if they find something of significance to the nation, they are obliged to protect the site.*

Hurrah! I thought. Then I gulped. National Heritage had had their chance, as far as I was concerned, but that wasn't why I'd gulped. I gulped because I hadn't emailed Alex the whole story. I'd sort of skipped the details about Robert Collins planning to build on the site. I'd kind of omitted to tell Alex about Mrs Collins going into a home. I'd definitely not made it completely clear that Drummer's field didn't exactly belong to me.

Why?

Well, you know what grown-ups are like, they always go on about knowing best. They will insist that you don't know how things work and that the most boring, stupid, unreasonable, unfair, idiotic and downright insane things are right in the eyes of the law and that's that. I had feared that if I'd I told Alex all the ins and outs of our situation, he wouldn't want to get involved.

But he did! It was totally brilliant that Alex had responded! Alex had contacts. Alex had come up trumps. Alex was on our side.

A celebrity, James had said we needed. Well, I'd come up with one. I'd played my celebrity joker, and he had turned out better than we had ever hoped. I'd done my bit. Now we all had to pray that Jessica Tamarad and *Time Detectives* would save the day.

It was our second chance.

Chapter Thirteen

Suddenly everything seemed to happen very fast.

Firstly, I got an email from Jessica Tamarad, asking to come and view the site. Everyone was instantly buoyed up by this news, of course.

"Brilliant!" shouted James. "Great work Pia. I didn't think anyone would really be able to get a celebrity, but you did."

"And you started the ball rolling with the TV thing. This is so going to work," Katy said.

Sophie was all for it. She also had a couple of reservations, though. "Did you tell them who the site belonged to, Pia?" she asked me.

Uh-oh, I thought, here we go . . .

"Er, well I didn't actually say," I told her. "She didn't actually ask."

"Good!" Sophie said, decisively. "No point putting

up barriers until the TV show is ready to take the bait. We have to play this thing with a bit of cunning."

I could see Katy looking doubtful. She's always up-front about things but I was with Sophie on this one. After all, things were getting desperate and this was our second chance. We couldn't blow it now. I told Sophie Jessica Tamarad was coming on Saturday, in two days' time.

"Oh, that's not good!" Sophie said. "Dee and I have a show – miles away. We won't be here."

"Don't worry," Katy said, "we'll all be here and show her round."

"OK, get her drooling over what she might find," Sophie advised us.

"Got it!" I'd told her, pushing away the nagging worry that had crept into my gut again. We had to do this!

Secondly, Aunt P came over again to – in her words – sort her darling Bam-Bam. We were all dreading it – no one more so than poor Bambi.

"So tell me," Bambi said, her voice heavy with sarcasm, "am I supposed to let myself be sorted out, or not? You're the people with all the smart ideas. That don't work," she added.

"What's she saying?" asked Cat. I told her.

"What's the answer?" I asked. Everyone stayed silent.

"I suppose . . ." began Katy, ". . . it depends on how, exactly, Aunt P intends to do the sorting."

"That's helpful, not!" said Bambi. I relayed this back to the waiting gang.

"You'll have to play it by ear," said Cat, laying her pink cheek against her pony's brown one. "I can't bear the thought of you going back to Aunt Pam's, but I don't want Aunt Pam getting rough with you. You'll have to decide for yourself what will be worth doing."

Bambi stayed silent.

I'd got Drummer in from the field and he was in his stable next door. I didn't want him leaning over the gate and encouraging Bambi. Whatever Bambi did, it had to be her decision. She had to make up her own mind how far to go.

"I can't even have a go at Aunt Pam," moaned Cat. "Bambi belongs to her, not me."

"If she's really horrible, we could always call the horse charities," said Bean.

"She won't be cruel," Cat told her, pulling a face. "She's not a monster."

"I'm very glad to hear that!" Bambi murmured.

"Look out, she's here!" shouted Dee, and we all piled

out of Bambi's stable and scattered.

"I can't bear to look," said Katy, disappearing into Bluey's stable with a broom. "I'm going to de-cobweb Bluey's stable."

"That should take you all of three minutes," observed Bean. Katy's stable was immaculate. "Why don't you do Tiffany's instead? That will keep you busy for ages."

"Because it's your job, and you're just too lazy to do it!" replied Katy.

Cat held Aunt Pam's offside stirrup as she mounted up in the yard. The tension in Bambi was obvious for all to see. Her head was up, her tail clamped down and she rolled her eyes to try to see what Aunt Pam was up to in her saddle.

"She's got a whacking great long schooling whip!" whispered Bean.

"Whacking?" I asked. "That's a poor choice of word."

"Don't!" Bean said.

"Poor Bambi!" cried Katy.

Aunt Pam headed Bambi for the school and Cat joined us, her face as black as thunder. "If she hurts Bambi," she said, her hands clenched into fists, "I'll, I'll . . ."

I gulped. This was so not good.

For a few moments we all stood in silence. Well, almost.

"Must you do that?" cried Katy, looking daggers at Bean.

"What?"

"Bite your nails?"

"They're my nails!"

"I can hear you crunching. It's disgusting!"

"You're in a right mood today!"

"I'm stressed!"

Bean looked skyward and stuffed her hands in her pockets.

We stood about not saying anything, seeing as everything anyone said just fired up everyone else. The moments ticked by.

"She's back!" yelled Cat, bounding out of the stable as Bambi returned to the yard with a clatter of hoof beats. Aunt Pam was no longer in the saddle. Handing the reins over to Cat, we saw her say something – and by her body language, it wasn't complimentary. Fingers were pointed at Bambi, then wagged at Cat as Cat's face turned redder and redder.

Eventually, Aunt Pam got in her car and whizzed off, and we all poured out of our hiding place now the enemy had retreated.

"What happened?" I demanded.

"That showed her!" Bambi said, adding a *humph!* At the end.

"Aunt Pam's furious!" Cat told us, miserably.

"Why?" asked Katy.

"Because," said Bambi, defiantly, "I sorted her out!"

"Bambi dumped her," Cat explained. "She's not a happy bunny."

"What did she say?" Bean asked. "Is she giving up her idea of having Bambi at home?"

"Oh yes," Cat said, nodding, "she's decided Bambi's far too naughty for Emily after all."

"Hurrah!" yelled Bean, punching the air. "Our plan worked brilliantly!"

I looked at Katy. She looked back at me. Something wasn't right.

"You don't look very happy about it, Cat," I said. She looked anything but.

Throwing her arms around Bambi's neck, Cat began to cry. Bambi lowered her head and nuzzled Cat's back in sympathy.

"I overdid it, didn't I?" Bambi said, quietly.

"Are you crying with joy?" Bean asked her, hopefully.

"No!" came Cat's muffled reply. "Not only has Aunt Pam decided she doesn't want Bambi at home any more, she's decided she doesn't want her *at all*."

"But that was the plan," said Katy, confused. "That's what you wanted – for Aunt Pam to continue letting you have her on loan."

"You don't understand," Cat told us, between sniffs. "She isn't going to let me have her. Aunt Pam is going to sell Bambi!"

Chapter Fourteen

Saturday dawned bright, sunny and warm. So why did I keep shivering?

"What time is it?" James asked me, for about the millionth time.

"Haven't you got a watch?" I asked him, crossly. Nerves were so getting to me, I thought.

"I use my mobile," he explained.

"Well you're not using it now!" I snapped. I'd lost count of the number of times I'd glanced down the drive, looking for Jessica Tamarad's car, even though I knew she wasn't due for another hour.

Everyone but Sophie and Dee were at the yard. Mrs Bradley was being dragged around, as usual, by her bolshy Dales pony. Nicky was keeping an eye on her daughter Bethany, who was dabbing her pony Pippin with a dandy brush while Pippin dozed in the sun. I think he was actually snoring. Cat had gone riding on Bambi. She had said she didn't know how many more times she'd be able to do that and she wanted to be alone.

Drummer wasn't speaking to me. He wasn't speaking to me because of Aunt Pam's plans for Bambi. He felt I'd let him down (and I could see his point) so I was getting the silent treatment. He pretended he was angry, but really, I think he didn't trust himself to speak. He was awfully upset and I had no words to console him. That was partly why I was being so ratty with James.

I looked along the drive again and there was a car, coming along it.

"She's early!" I thought, getting up to greet her. James came out of Moth's stable and stood by my side as the car stopped and out got the driver, wearing cords and a dark-coloured shirt.

"She's one unattractive woman," murmured James, snorting.

I gasped. When I breathed out, it came out in a single word. "Oh!"

"Hi Pia!" said Alex Willard, waving at me as he slammed the car door shut.

"Er, hello," I replied.

123

"You didn't expect to see me, did you?" asked the great man, grinning, "but I thought I'd come along and see if I could do anything. I'd hate to see you all get evicted because of new developments here."

"Oh thanks," I gushed, "thanks very, very much."

"I thought I'd stay for a few days and see what Jessica finds. It's going to be pretty exciting."

I was confused. It sounded like Jessica was arriving with a shovel and was going to start digging today. I thought she was just having a look-see.

Everyone suddenly came out of the woodwork, anxious to be introduced to the famous horseman. Alex remembered Bean from when we'd gone to his yard on our riding holiday, and he said he remembered James and Katy, too, from our activity ride, but he was lovely to Mrs Bradley, who went all shy and giggly (so not a good idea – she's too ancient for that kind of behaviour), and Nicky was just as bad.

"He's *soooo* good looking," she whispered to me, when Alex was talking to Katy. I supposed he was, in an old sort of way. I mean, he's got grey hair and everything, he must be at least forty.

And then Jessica Tamarad turned up.

After what seemed like hours of chatting between Jessica and Alex, we finally all trooped out to the field to look at where the house used to be, all standing looking at the grass and the trees which hid the view behind them.

"So this is it, then?" Jessica asked. She had long black hair and dark eyes and she was wearing a pair of jeans and a white shirt. A huge yellow gemstone swung from a long golden chain around her neck and her fingers held a collection of golden rings. She could give Sophie a run for her money in the glamour stakes.

We all stared at the ground and nodded.

"We've surveyed the site from the air," Jessica said, smiling, "and it's come up trumps."

"That's fantastic," said Alex, grinning at me.

"From the air?" I asked.

"Yes," said Jessica, "we can see whether there has been a structure from the air – this site shows a huge house used to be here. Definitely Elizabethan."

"How on earth can you know?" asked Katy.

"From the shape. Most big houses built at that time were in the shape of a letter E. The aerial shots show such a house. It's very exciting!"

It certainly was!

"National Heritage didn't think so," grumbled Bean.

"Well, we're certain we'll find lots of interesting things once we start digging," Jessica said, firmly. "I've got the team coming first thing Monday morning to get cracking."

"What?" we all yelled.

"Oh yes, all sorted," said Jessica, looking around.

"It will be fascinating to see what you do find," agreed Alex.

"Er, there's just one thing about that," I said, nervously biting the inside of my mouth. "The land doesn't actually, well technically, sort of belong to us and . . ."

"Oh, I know that," Jessica said, flicking her long black hair over her shoulder with one hand. "I've already arranged with the owner for us to bring in the machinery and tents. We pay them, of course."

We all stood there, totally lost for words.

"You've spoken to Mrs Collins?" asked Dee.

"*Mr* Collins," corrected Jessica. "I've been dealing with Mr Robert Collins. He said I was to deal directly with him. We can't do anything without the owner's permission, naturally!"

"Oh," I said. Obviously, Robert Collins had already forced his mother to hand over the stables to him. "And he agreed to you digging up the site?" I asked, wanting to be sure.

"Oh yes, very helpful," said Jessica.

"Why?" James asked. "Won't you want to preserve the site, if you find what you are looking for?"

"Well, that's debatable . . ." Jessica began.

I didn't like where this was going.

". . . we are hoping to find some artefacts," she continued, "but obviously the structure is no more. I mean, it's not like we can open a house to the public – but I'm sure whatever we find will be of great historical interest."

"She's no better than National stinking Heritage!" James whispered in my ear.

"Shhhh!" I whispered back, unable to believe my ears.

"So you wouldn't stop Robert Collins building on the land once you've finished finding whatever you hope to find?" Alex asked.

"We can't really," Jessica confirmed. "I mean, it's his land."

"He's getting you to dig the foundations for his houses!" James exploded.

"Probably!" Jessica laughed. "I wouldn't be surprised!"

"And you're paying him!" cried Dee.

"Yes," agreed Jessica. "Ironic, isn't it?"

"It's *criminal*!" burst out Katy.

Alex looked at me with a sorry-didn't-know-about-this kind of look and I felt sick.

"Oh great!" exploded James. "We're actually *helping* Robert Collins. We've played right into his hands!"

"Now we've got to come up with a *third* chance!" wailed Katy, to the bewilderment of both Alex and Jessica. "Because our second chance is total rubbish!

Chapter Fifteen

When I told mum that Alex Willard was staying in the area for a few days, she immediately said we should all meet up for dinner at the pub.

"He won't know anyone here, it's only polite and he is trying to help you after all, Pia," she'd told me, when I'd explained why he was here.

I remembered the first meeting Mum had had with Alex Willard and wasn't keen to repeat the experience. Mum flirting. Alex embarrassed. Me wanting to die. Then I remembered the second meeting they'd had. Alex had definitely been interested in my mum on that occasion.

An idea started growing in my brain. What if . . . ?

"I'll give him a call on his mobile," I said.

"How come you've got Alex Willard's mobile number?" Mum asked me, suspiciously.

I waved his card at her and she narrowed her eyes. "I thought you said you'd lost that?" she said, in an accusing way.

I shrugged my shoulders. "I thought I had!" I lied. I'd told her that because I'd been scared she'd ring him for a date. Now, with my new idea, I wasn't so sure that hiding it had been such a good idea.

Alex was dead chuffed to be invited. I told him the name of the pub, and where it was and we agreed to all be there at seven.

The Mill House is a fabulous, tiny, old pub with great food and as it is only half a mile away from where we live, Mum and I walked there. Alex had already found a table and was waiting with a bottle of chilled white wine, two glasses and a Coke for me. Mum and Alex greeted each other – *Hi Sue, you look terrific: Hello Alex, we couldn't let you eat on your own now could we?* – while I watched intently. Was there still a spark there on Alex's side? He'd definitely shown interest in Mum at the activity ride at Christmas. Mum had been well keen on Alex when we'd first seen him at the TV studios. Did they still find each other attractive?

Because here was my plan:

Get Alex to fancy my mum.

Get my mum to fancy Alex.

Get them to hook up.

Live happily ever after.

I mean how cool would it be having Alex Willard as a step dad? No, really! Imagine!

As we sat and Mum and Alex chatted, my plan seemed to be going great guns. They laughed, they drank some wine (my mum didn't drink too much like she did the first time they met – thus proving to Alex that she wasn't some kind of binge drinker gone bananas), and they seemed very interested in each other.

"Where are you staying, Alex?" asked my mum.

"At Holly House B+B, about four doors down from here," Alex replied.

"I didn't know there was a B+B in the village," I said.

"Pia, you never notice anything unless it involves horses," my mum told me, lifting her eyebrows at Alex in a knowing way.

I opened my mouth to protest, but then shut it again. She'd got me bang to rights on that one.

"Oh, there's Mike – yoo-hoo Mike, over here!" yelled my mum as Mike-the-bike strolled into the bar in his motorcycle leathers. What was he doing here?

My mum (dippy as she is) had apparently told him

to join us. This was a major blow to my plan. Was it my imagination or did Alex look disappointed when Mike walked in? Apparently not, as before long, Mike and Alex were yakking on like old mates – about motorbikes, can you believe? *V-Twin* this and *suspension* that. I felt myself come over all sulky.

"Whatever are they going on about?" I asked Mum. "Motorbike talk is so boring."

"That's how we feel when you start up about horses," my mum replied, rather harshly, I thought. And she looked all smug like she'd scored a major victory. Honestly, parents! The thought that she might not take too well to a horsey person did cross my mind, but I decided she'd get used to it. After all, she got used to Mike's motorbike. If she could ride on the back of that, she could surely ride a horse. I imagined my mum riding, getting really into it. That would be good, wouldn't it? Providing she didn't morph into someone like Dee's mum, Sophie. I decided I'd have to keep an eye on that.

The rest of the evening went either terrifically well, or very disappointingly, depending on your point of view. Alex, Mike and my Mum seemed to have a whale of a time but my plan to get Mum off with Alex was a complete failure. I would have to think up another way to get them together without Mike, I decided. And then, my plan was initiated without my help.

"Are you staying here long, Alex?" Mum asked him.

Alex assured her that he was and Mum suggested we all got together for another meal at The Mill House in a few days' time To which Mike said he couldn't because he was having a night out with the lads from work but that shouldn't stop us from going ahead, so Mum and Alex agreed to meet up without him. Result! I felt slightly guilty at Mike being so good about it – after all, he was the best boyfriend Mum had found so far by miles and MILES and here he was, helping my plan to get him replaced with Alex Willard, horse trainer extraordinaire.

I calmed my conscience by telling myself that maybe my mum was interested in Alex again after all. I mean, *she'd* thought of meeting up again without any prompting from me. Maybe my plan had a chance of working. At last, I thought, as we walked home, something seemed to be going right.

It was about time!

Chapter Sixteen

By the time we all got to the yard on Monday evening after school, the Time Detectives had got cracking! The area in the field where the house had been had been roped off, a huge great chunk of turf had been cut out by a bulldozer and three student-types and an older man with long white hair and a beard were raking around with trowels and brushes, while a camera crew filmed a man and a woman who asked questions and got over-excited whenever anyone found a brick or a piece of anything that wasn't dirt. Jessica and a tall, lanky bald man were wandering about with clipboards and drinking coffee out of polystyrene cups. Several vans were also within the roped off area. Everyone had been very excited at the thought of a film crew at the yard, but once we'd got used to the idea it was actually very boring – nothing much seemed to happen – and they seemed to film it not happening all the time.

The ponies had spent all day in their stables. Considering the sacrifice was all about them, they were taking it very badly.

"WHY am I confined to barracks?" Drum demanded to know, as soon as I turned up.

"I take it you're talking to me again," I replied, snootily. My sympathy had changed to annoyance after he had blanked me for days.

"Never mind that – what's going on?"

I told him – missing out the bit about our plan not going entirely as we had wanted and it being unlikely that we'd actually saved the stables but instead helped Robert Collins's start on the foundations for his buildings. So Drummer softened a bit. Only a bit.

When I walked across the yard to the barn, Bambi wanted to know the same thing. Moth was her usual quiet self – thank goodness – Bluey asked me politely and Tiffany just stood at the back of her stable, her eyes all wide and anxious. The noise of the bulldozers and camera crew traffic all day had put her on edge. Or possibly over it. Dolly was lying down and catching up on some zeds, having been to a big show the day before. She wasn't the least bit interested, being out for the count and barred from the field anyway. Besides, she encountered all sorts of strange things at county shows every weekend.

My mobile went – and the number calling wasn't on top of my list of favourites right now. I pushed the button anyway and put the phone to my ear.

"Hi Dad!" I said, making a pretty good job of sounding pleased to hear him.

"Hi Pia!" Dad shouted back. At last, I thought, he'd stopped called me Pumpkin. That was one good thing.

"Lyn and I are very excited about the possibility of moving near to you – Laurel Heights is an amazing location. We'll be able to see much more of you. Why, Drummer and us, we'd be neighbours – or *neigh*-bours! Get it? Ha ha!"

I got it. That joke was at least two centuries old and it hadn't been funny when it had been wheeled out the first time. For all I knew, it was the cause of Queen Victoria telling everyone that she was not amused. Neither was I.

"Actually Dad," I began, intending to put him straight about Drummer being threatened with eviction due to building works, but Dad talked over me.

"Listen, don't get your hopes up, Pumpkin . . ." my heart sank. There was no chance of my hopes getting up, nothing ever seemed to go right – even my pumpkin crusade. ". . . but I know Lyn's very keen on the plot."

"OK, I won't," I said, meekly.

"Anyway Pia, when are we going to see you? Soon I hope!"

"Er, things are a bit hectic at the moment, Dad," I replied, crossing my fingers behind my back in preparation for the lies to come. As it happened, I didn't need them. Dad didn't want specific dates, he was just talking the talk. After a few more moments of talking about school and how I was getting on, he rang off, leaving me more despondent than ever about the proposed development.

"Was that your Dad?" asked Drummer. I nodded. "Can't wait to shove us all off so he can live here?"

"In a nutshell!" I told him.

"Won't come to that," Drummer assured me.

"How can you possibly know?" I wailed. I could see it all: Skinny Lynny parking her red sports car in the car port where Drummer's stable now stood. Walking over to her house, our barn (converted), her high heels clicking on the path, picking a rose from around the door and sighing at the countryness of it all. My shoulders slumped with hopelessness.

"I'm telling you," said Drummer, "it will never happen. You mark my words."

I wanted to believe him.

I just couldn't.

Chapter Seventeen

I had such high hopes for dinner with my mum and Alex at the pub on Tuesday, I could hardly sit still. This was so going to work! Why hadn't I thought of it before? I could so get my mum a suitable boyfriend. More suitable than the ones she picked herself, although I was a bit troubled by my casual discarding of Mike-the-bike. He was definitely her best boyfriend yet and I still had pangs of guilt at the thought of him being dumped. But think of the bigger picture! Alex Willard as a step-dad. Hello!

Mum and I got to the pub first and as we waited for Alex to arrive I fiddled with the menu. I fidgeted. I kept sighing. In the end, Mum told me I was getting on her nerves and to act my age.

"Honestly, Pia, that Lhasa Apso over there is better behaved than you," she said, tutting.

"It's a Shih Tzu, actually," I mumbled, throwing the menu on to the table and sighing again. Just before Mum got all heavy about attitude someone came through the door and saved me. "Oh, there's Alex!" I cried, leaping up.

Air kisses were exchanged. Got to improve on that, I thought.

We all sat down and Alex and my mum started talking like they were old friends. I couldn't believe how well things were going. I even heard my mum ask whether anyone was missing Alex at home (how transparent!) and how long he'd known Jessica, and he assured her he had no-one at home and told her that he had known Jessica and *her husband* (phew, I was worried there for a minute) for some time. My mum seemed pleased too. I mean, it was all working out perfectly and I could just tell Mum still fancied Alex. She looked so thrilled once she'd established that Alex was a free agent. I felt almost like I had a placard to wave which said *Alex Willard for Pia's Step-dad*! I could hardly sit still I was so excited about how well things were panning out.

And then, of course, we had a reality check. Big time.

"Hiya Suze!" a shrill voice pierced the air and the

Lhasa Apso, Shih Tzu, whatever, leapt in the air and started barking hysterically like a siren had gone off.

Oh poo, poo, poo! I thought, my heart sinking. Would nothing I organise ever go right?

"Carol!" exclaimed my mum, feigning surprise very badly.

Yeah, right! I thought. You don't fool me. It was totally obvious she'd tipped her dreadful man-eating friend Carol off and got her to come along. What for, I did not know. It wasn't long, though, before things began to fall into place.

"You must be Alex!" gushed Carol, smiling so widely it was like a black hole opening up and I thought we were all going to get sucked into it and disappear forever. She swung her ample chest in Alex's direction, followed by the rest of her. As far as her skimpy pink crossover top went, there was more of Carol out than in, and I couldn't tell whether Alex was startled or impressed.

"You must join us," insisted Mum, unable to keep the smugness out of her voice as she pulled up another chair next to Alex for her friend.

I wasn't the only one with plans, I thought. It was becoming obvious where I'd inherited my scheming ways. There I was trying to set my mum up with Alex, and here she was trying to set him up with Carol. Not that Carol needed anyone's help – she never did. All flashing eyes, cleavage and teeth, she brushed Alex's arm throughout the meal, hung on his every word and laughed like a drain whenever he said anything remotely amusing. It was as though someone, somewhere, had decided that whatever I tried to do, they were going to make sure it didn't happen. Furiously I tore my paper napkin to shreds under the table and got more and more annoyed. If this was karma, I must have done something terrible.

I took myself off to the loo to beat the walls in frustration and have a good scream. Only I couldn't do that either because there were two women in there plastering on the slap and bitching about their so-called friend they'd left at the table. My leaden feet dragged me back to the scene of disappointment where Alex was telling my mum and Carol all about the Time Detectives' dig and their latest research, which was much more interesting than listening to Carol's alternate hysterical and inane ramblings.

"I thought it was an Elizabethan house?" my mum asked. What had I missed, I thought.

Alex nodded and gulped down some wine. "Yes, the one Jessica is most interested in was built around 1600, but there was another house built to the right of it in 1750, after a fire destroyed the first one. The same family built and lived in both – well, generations of the same family, I mean."

Carol went off into one of her over-the-top laughs which made everything on her shudder, which made me shudder. Mum leant forward and urged Alex to continue. She seemed fascinated – and so was I. This was far more interesting than listening to Carol wittering on, even if I was in the depths of despair over my failed plan.

"Yes," repeated Alex, "generations of the same family. They're all buried in the church in the village. It used to be their family church, apparently. They built it."

"What, St Mark's?" asked my mum.

"If that's what it's called," nodded Alex. "They fill about a quarter of the graveyard, so I'm told. Well, their remains do."

I shuddered again.

"What was their name?" asked Mum.

Alex frowned. "Hmmm, can't remember, something to do with boats. It's all in the local and church records, Jessica has had her researchers finding out as much as they can. Apparently, one of the early ancestors married a duchess, another one made a lot of money in the colonies and there was a bit of a scandal with two of the sons after the First World War. There were four sons originally, but two died in the trenches in France. The eldest of those left was due to inherit the estate but the youngest made a lot of noise about it not being fair and wanting half of it. Anyway, the eldest solved that particular argument by secretly running off with one of the girls in the village and was never seen again.

"Oh, how romantic!" gushed Carol, clutching her chest in a demonstration of how much she was moved by the story.

"So who got the money?" asked Mum.

"Well, it doesn't have a happy ending I'm afraid," Alex continued. "The second son was a gambler – which was why he was so keen to get hold of the inheritance – and had already run up huge debts. According to Jessica's researchers, the old man had never wanted his younger son to inherit and there was talk of him considering leaving his estate to a cousin, but he died before he could change his will so the younger son inherited after all."

"Sounds suspicious," said Carol, smacking her lips together in morbid glee. I had to agree with her on this one. Well suspicious!

"I bet the younger son did the father in!" Carol added, her eyes shining.

"What happened then?" asked Mum, leaning forward.

"The son continued to gamble, continued to lose, running up more and more debts and eventually he died in poverty, the end of the family line. There were rumours that he went mad in the end, running through the empty house yelling and cursing."

"Guilt!" cried Carol, triumphantly. "Guilt drove him barking!"

"Why didn't he sell the house?" asked Mum, not keen on sensationalism.

"No-one wanted it, apparently," Alex explained, shrugging. "No money about just after the War. The house fell into disrepair and had to be demolished.

Wow, I thought, all that drama that had gone on in Drummer's field. No wonder Tiffany's a nervous wreck.

"That's a cheerful little story!" exclaimed my mum, sitting back and picking up the dessert menu. "How about something sweet to get us all smiling again?"

Good idea, I agreed. I might as well get something out of this evening, seeing as my master plan had gone down the drain.

Carol rubbed her hands together and grinned. "That was fascinating!" she told Alex. "Do you think the family's ghosts all haunt the area?"

"Don't be stupid Carol!" snapped Mum, glancing at me.

"Oh, sorry!" mumbled Carol, rolling her eyes. "There is no such thing as ghosts, you know that don't you, Pia? I was only joking!"

I gave her an indulgent smile and picked up my Coke. I decided I'd have lemon meringue pie. That would cheer me up.

"Oh, I remember what the family's name was," said Alex, clicking his fingers. "I knew it would come to me – it's not exactly to do with boats but you'll get the connection when I tell you."

"Well?" asked Carol, hanging on his every word. I sighed and took a swig of Coke.

"Rowe!" said Alex. "The family name was Rowe."

I spat Coke all over the table.

Chapter Eighteen

I couldn't wait to get to the yard the next day and tell everyone. To say I was freaked was an understatement – but how I felt was nothing compared to how Bean took the news.

"You mean that nutter we called up on the ouija board really existed?" she screeched at me, throwing her arms around like a windmill.

I knew she was a little bit upset, because she had Tiffany on the end of the lead rope, and she never, ever does anything around her pony that might upset her. Tiffany reminded her of this policy by throwing her head up and backing up across the yard in a frenzy, yelling, "What? What? What?"

"Oh Tiff, sorry, sorry, it's all right," soothed Bean, focusing on her pony and putting her own feelings on the back burner until Tiffany had calmed down and was convinced that nothing terrible was about to happen – for the time being anyway. Once Bean had put Tiffany in her stable, she turned on me again.

"Are you sure that's the name Alex gave you?" she asked, her face white.

"What's the conflab about?" said a voice. We both jumped about a mile in the air. Talk about edgy!

"Oh James, you scared us half to death!" scolded Bean.

"What? What did I do?" asked James, all innocent – which, of course, he was.

We explained. A low whistle escaped James. "That is so cool!" he said, grinning. "That Adam Rowe fellow, the one we got at the séance, moaning about his *bad death*, that must have been the dad. His younger son must have murdered him!"

"That's what Carol said," I told him.

"Who?"

"Never mind."

"I told you I wasn't pushing the beaker, didn't I?" said James.

I had already thought of that. So didn't want to.

Bean shuddered. "Stop it!"

"Oh Bean, it happened years and years ago," said James, his eyes glinting with the excitement of it all.

"It was only last summer!" protested Bean.

"I mean the Rowe family feud and possible bad death," explained James, giving me a look.

"Well it grosses me out!" Bean replied.

"And me," I admitted.

We couldn't wait to tell the others – not Cat, of course. Any mention of the séance and she got grumpy. I wished *I* didn't know about it. I'd gladly exchange freaked out for grumpy any day.

"So the old man got done in by his son, did he?" asked Katy. "How horrible!"

"That's a pretty bad death in my book," said Dee, ghoulishly. "This is so fantastic!"

"You're weird, do you know that?" said Bean, looking at her in amazement.

"Do you reckon he poisoned him?" I asked.

"Or smothered him with a pillow, like in that film," suggested Dee, still smiling.

"What film?"

"Can't remember its name. Old black and white job. The woman smothers the faithful old servant with a pillow and he's too weak to cry out. I bet that's what he did. No evidence, you see."

"Can you all *please* shut up?" asked Bean, hugging herself.

"Why did she kill off a faithful old servant?" asked James.

"Dunno," Dee replied, "I didn't see all of it, just that bit. She was evil, though."

"La la la la la la la," chanted Bean, her fingers in her ears.

Standing in front of her, James opened his eyes wide and made a slashing motion across his throat. Bean took one hand down to give James a shove, then put it back up to her exposed ear again.

"So they all lived in the big house?" asked Katy.

"According to Alex's story," I said. "And the family is buried in St Mark's churchyard."

"Let's go and look at the graves!" yelled Dee, jumping up.

"No way!"

"Get lost!"

"Don't think so!"

"What are you all saying?"

"Take your fingers out of your ears and you'll hear us!"

"Shhhh, here comes Cat. You know how she hates us talking about it," hissed Katy, as Cat came along the drive.

"What's going on?" asked Cat. "Why have you got

your fingers in your ears, Bean?"

"Oh, nothing," said James, winking at me. My knees went all wobbly. I hate myself, sometimes. I mean, it's so pathetic. "We're just talking about Laurel Heights, again!"

"Why have you got your fingers in your ears, Bean?" repeated Cat.

"Coming riding?" Katy asked her. "We're all going for a hack in the woods as it's so hot."

"Mmmm, OK. I'll get Bambi," said Cat. "But why has . . . ?"

Bean took her fingers out of her ears and narrowed her eyes. "Have you all finished?" she said, looking at us all.

James bundled her off to the barn, with Bean's protests drowned out by James telling her to come and get Tiffany's grooming kit – even though it was in the tackroom.

"What *is* going on?" asked Cat again.

"Oh, you know Bean!" said Katy, grinning and shrugging her shoulders, and we all fled to get the ponies ready for their ride.

We all had a great ride. Sophie was in a particularly mellow mood so Dee had been allowed to come with us, providing we all rode *sensibly*, Sophie had insisted, with a particularly threatening look. Of course, five minutes away from the yard *that* went out of the window when Dee suggested we all play cowboys and Indians. James, Cat and Bean were the Indians, and Katy, Dee and I were the cowboys, and we took it in turn to find each other after a 100-count start. It was a bit like hide-and-seek, only on ponies. James would insist on making whooping noises, which totally freaked out Tiffany, not that Bean seemed to care. She was too freaked out by the Rowe connection to worry about Tiffany bombing off through the trees.

Drummer loved it. He especially loved trying to find Bambi, which he did every time – which was annoying because I'd rather have found James. All the ponies, not just Tiff, got thoroughly over-excited and we had to walk them home to cool off and get them to settle.

"My mum will never let me come out with you all again if I take Dolly back in this state!" Dee warned us, as Dolly jogged along, fighting for her head and sweating, chanting, *Let's do it again!* over and over. "For goodness sake, Pia, have a word, will you?"

"It was your idea!" I mumbled, trying to convince Dolly to walk quietly.

By the time we got back to the yard the ponies were cool and – with the exception of Tiffany – walking calmly. Jessica was in the yard with Alex, and she had news.

"What is it?" we asked eagerly, crowding around her on the ponies.

"Have you found anything?" asked Katy.

"Yes, we've found lots of things," said Jessica, "but the foundations alone, although fascinating, won't help your cause, I'm afraid."

"But if they're so fascinating, why don't you want to preserve them?" asked Bean.

"I'm sorry everyone," Jessica said, ruefully shaking her head, "but our work here is almost done and although we have put together a fabulous programme – and I have you all to thank for that – there is not much else we need. We'll be shooting the final few shots in the next couple of days and we'll probably be gone by the end of the week."

"Is there really no way whatsoever you can prevent Robert Collins from building here?" James asked, passionately. "Surely this Elizabethan house is important enough to stop any building work?"

"I'd love to say yes, James," Jessica replied, "really I would, but although National Heritage did show some initial interest in our discoveries, they're really not sufficiently interested in mere foundations. There's nothing to see, nothing to save."

"It's all been for nothing!" Bean hissed at me.

I didn't reply. I didn't trust myself to speak. In my mind I saw all the ponies being led into trailers and horseboxes and going off in different directions to new homes. I thought of never seeing Bean or Katy or Dee or even Cat again. I couldn't bring myself to imagine going to a yard where James wasn't.

"If only you had something here that was still intact," Jessica continued, smiling at James. "You know, a folly or a summer house or something. Anything that would tie in with the historical connections of this place and provide National Heritage with something tangible to latch on to."

"She means charge people to see," Bean whispered.

"There's the ice house," said James.

The ice house. Of course! I looked at Bean. She looked at me. We both looked at the others.

"The ice house!" we all chorused.

"There's an ice house?" Jessica asked him, sharply.

James nodded. "About a mile away. Next to the lake – obviously."

"Ice houses were usually later than Elizabethan," said Jessica, "but I'd be very interested to see it. They're fascinating."

"So how old would it be?" asked Katy.

"Probably eighteenth century," Jessica said. "Can you show me tomorrow?"

"Of course!" I said, my heart soaring. Could the ice house really help us?

It was our third chance.

Chapter Nineteen

We were all at the yard bright and early, the ponies in and saddled, ready for the off. Then we had to wait around for Jessica and Alex. They arrived eventually, and with both of them walking, and all of us riding, we set off. Of course, with two pedestrians, it took ages to get there but we finally rode past the river and on to the clearing where the ice house was hidden.

As we approached, I felt my stomach churning with a mixture of excitement and fear. The ice house was such a spooky place. For a start, you would never find it if you didn't know it was there, it was set in a small clearing surrounded by trees and thick bushes, like it was hiding. When you did force your way through the leaves and branches, all you could see on three sides was a small, grassy mound. The fourth side held an old wooden door with big rusty hinges and looked for all

the world like a hobbit house. The creaking wood
door opened up into a dark, brick-lined space whi
dropped away below ground and into darkness. Before
refrigeration, ice would have been cut from the frozen
lake nearby in winter and stored in its cold depths,
ready to be used for ices and desserts in the big house
subsequently built next to the remains of the
Elizabethan mansion.

For something used for such a mundane purpose,
the ice house always gave me the creeps. It had been the
hiding place of Jazz, the traveller girl I'd befriended,
and Bambi had been held captive there, but even
without these connections the place just seemed (to
me, anyway) to have a sinister air about it. Hidden in
a clearing, few people seemed to know it even existed.

Why hadn't we thought of the ice house before?

Jessica and Alex didn't seem to have any qualms
about its spookiness. They loved it.

"Oh, wow!" exclaimed Jessica, tugging at the door
with Alex. "It's fantastic!"

They both disappeared inside while we sat on the
ponies in the sunshine.

"Will we be here long?" asked Bambi. She didn't like
being there – for obvious reasons, it brought back
unwelcome memories for her.

"It's OK, Bambi," I heard Drummer tell her, "we're all here with you."

"I hate this place, too," said Tiffany, looking around for an excuse to bolt home.

"Yes, well, we all know why," said Bluey, "but it happened a long time ago."

"What did?" I asked him.

"What did what?" everyone chorused at me.

"I was talking to Bluey," I explained.

Bluey didn't answer.

"What happened a long time ago, Bluey?" I repeated. Bluey just wrinkled up his muzzle and looked uncomfortable.

"Best you don't know," said Drummer, in the same sort of voice grown-ups use when they don't want to tell you something about a wayward aunt who's got lots of boyfriends, or why they'd fallen out with the neighbours. It's bad enough when they do it, without having to put up with the same sort of thing from my own pony. Annoying? I think so!

Alex and Jessica returned, interrupting my thoughts.

"This is fabulous!" Jessica enthused. "I'll find out whose land this is and then I can get the team along to take a look. I mean, there probably won't be anything much to discover but it's such a well-preserved ice house, it will make an interesting recording."

"You mean it won't help to stop the development?" asked Katy, getting straight to the point.

"I can't see how it could," Alex told us. "It's so far away from it."

"There goes our third chance," grumbled Bean.

I felt disappointed for another reason. I hadn't really wanted to draw attention to the ice house, it was sort of the yard secret. Who knew what would happen to it once everyone knew it was there. It would be labelled as dangerous and fenced off. We'd never be able to come and see it again. Not that I particularly wanted to, but it was sort of special, something we knew about that no-one else did.

We all trooped back to the yard, feeling down, and it wasn't until I was in bed that night that I remembered we still hadn't found out what the ponies knew about the ice house. I remember deciding just before I fell asleep that I'd tackle Drum about it the next day. Only the next day so much happened, the ice house was the last thing on my mind.

Chapter Twenty

When I arrived at the yard, everything was in uproar, as usual. The Time Detectives were getting in everyone's way, leaving the hose running and parking their cars in stupid places (like right across the entrance to the barn or the outdoor school), and I noticed that James was leaning over Bambi's stable door, talking to Catriona, which was odd, given their attitude to each other since they'd been out together and split up.

I parked my bike and tried to look nonchalant as I walked up to Drum's stable to get his headcollar.

"Here's Pia," announced James, "she'll be able to help."

"Help with what?" I asked, sidling up beside James and peering into Bambi's stable. Our combined silhouettes blocked most of the daylight but as I looked into the gloom it was obvious that Cat and

Bambi were not happy.

"Someone is coming to see Bambi," said Cat, her voice trembling as she threw the saddle on her skewbald mare.

At first, being a bit dim, I didn't get the significance of what she was telling me. Coming to see Bambi? That was nice. And then I did get it. Wham! I got it all right. How dim was I?

"Oh no!" I cried, my hand flying to my mouth in horror. "You mean, coming to try her? To buy her?"

"That's exactly what she means!" said James, grimly.

"So much for all your bright ideas!" grumbled Bambi, snaking her head up and down as Cat did up her girth. "Now I'm going to the highest bidder, shipped off to goodness-only-knows where, with some people I don't know, with ponies I'm not chummy with, leaving Drummer – and it's all YOUR FAULT!"

"Mine?" I protested.

"Not just yours – everyone!" moaned Bambi – with some justification. I was relieved to hear that I wasn't held personally responsible. I usually seemed to be. But then, I thought, this isn't about me, it's about Bambi. Whatever could we do now?

We heard a car door slam – Katy had arrived. As her mum drove away Katy came over and we told her the bad news.

"Oh no!" she cried, her eyes wide, her mouth open. "We have to do something!"

"You've all done quite enough already!" snapped Bambi, as Cat did up the throatlatch to her bridle.

"Who's coming to try her?" asked James.

"Some girl who wants a second pony," spat out Cat, her eyes blazing. "Seems she's grown out of her first pony and wants something with a bit of go, a bit of a challenge which, thanks to our plan being so successful, Bambi is now deemed to be."

"Well that's easy to remedy," said James, casually. "I mean, Bambi just has to be the opposite of what the girl wants."

Everyone was silent. This plan was brilliant in its simplicity. Bambi now had to be boringly quiet.

Bambi sighed. "OK, so now you want me to be a slowcoach, am I getting that right?"

"Perfectly!" I told her, and explained to the others that Bambi had it sussed.

"Well I, for one, am getting well confused!" snapped Cat.

"Isn't that your Aunt Pam's car?" asked Katy, gazing down the drive.

We all scattered, leaving Cat and Bambi to it. From

162

the safety of the tackroom we watched as Aunt Pam went into Bambi's stable to brief Cat. Then another car arrived, a huge 4X4, ejecting a tall, blonde woman and a girl a bit younger than us, dressed in a polo shirt and jodhpurs and looking excited.

"Bambi's just about to ruin her day!" remarked James.

"Oh, what a shame," said Katy, kindly. "What's more exciting than looking for a pony?"

"She's the enemy!" I growled, unsympathetic to anyone wanting to take Bambi away from my Drummer. I was glad he was still in the field – I could only guess his reaction to this latest development in our Bambi saga.

We sat on tackboxes in the tackroom, pretending we weren't interested, yet looked intently at proceedings in the yard. Cat led Bambi out while Aunt Pam talked to the woman and her daughter. We could hear her assuring them how Bambi was anything but a novice ride. The daughter smiled at Cat. Cat scowled back at her.

"We want something Natasha can do all Pony Club activities on," the mother said, as Natasha stroked Bambi's nose, "and she needs a pony with some go in it. Our old Sunshine is too slow for Nat these days." Cat just stood there, holding her beloved Bambi while her pony's merits were discussed in front of her. I could only imagine how she was feeling. This was just terrible!

"Catriona will ride Bambi, first," we heard Aunt Pam say, taking Bambi's reins so Cat could get her riding hat. She walked over to us in the tackroom, her face expressionless.

"Oh Cat," wailed Katy, "this is torture!"

"Tell me about it!" snapped Cat, jamming on her hat and retracing her steps. Mounting Bambi (Bambi stood in the yard with her head down, the very picture of a tired, dead-quiet, bored pony), Cat nudged her pony into a walk and the sorry party made their way to the outdoor school. We all trailed behind at a respectable distance, loitering by the barn, watching from afar.

There was a hold-up while Aunt Pam had to get one of the Time Detectives team to move their car by the school gate and Cat explained to Bambi's potential buyers about the TV series excavating the field, and then she was riding Bambi around the school. A very reluctant Bambi. A Bambi who looked barely able to put one hoof in front of the other.

"I wish we could hear what was being said!" I cried,

anxiously biting the inside of my cheek.

"Oh I can't bear it!" squeaked Katy. "This is just too awful!"

"That Bambi is one hell of an equine actress," observed James. She was, too.

"You don't have to hear what's being said to realise that Aunt Pam is pretty annoyed," I said. Cat's Aunt had her lips pressed together and her hands on her hips. I couldn't blame her, it must have been very confusing; one minute Bambi was all over the place like a pin-ball machine, the next she made like the quietest pony on the planet. Analyse that, I thought.

After just a few minutes demonstrating that Bambi wasn't going to do anything wild, Cat brought her to a halt (she was practically there anyway), dismounted and helped Natasha to mount, shortening her stirrups to the new rider's length.

"Is there anything Natasha needs to know about riding Bambi?" her mother asked. Cat shook her head, sulkily.

"Only that she's not right for you!" hissed James.

"Shhhh!" said Katy.

It took a while for Natasha to actually get Bambi going. Bambi did a great impression of a nappy pony refusing to go away from the gate and then, when she finally did, she kept cutting the corners of the school, walking in a circle rather than a large oblong. We heard Natasha's mother call out for Natasha to ride more positively, but Bambi was having none of it. She lumbered into a shuffling trot, then a reluctant canter, all the while keeping her head down and trying to slow down at every opportunity. She looked the perfect first pony, whereas Natasha wanted a second one. When Aunt Pam had ridden her, Bambi had acted more like a fourth or fifth pony – anything but a first one. Confusing? I'd say!

When Aunt Pam and Cat hauled in some jump wings and some poles, Bambi – who usually enjoys jumping – slowed down to a stop in front of the tiniest cross pole.

Natasha's mother had seen enough. After only five minutes in the saddle, Bambi's potential new rider was dismounted, back in the 4X4 and departing down the drive in a dust cloud of disappointment.

"Victory is ours!" declared Katy.

"Phew!" I sighed, relaxing a bit.

"That was the easy bit," muttered James, and we watched as Aunt Pam's head bobbed about in annoyance and frustration as she subjected Cat to a right old ear-bashing.

"She knows something's up," James said, ruefully. "She can't possibly know what, but she's suspicious all right."

"She can't be," Katy said, shaking her head. "How could she possibly suspect?"

But she did.

"Aunt Pam is furious!" Cat told us once her aunt had followed Natasha and her mum's wheel tracks off the yard. "Natasha's mother actually accused her of drugging Bambi and Aunt Pam told me she knew I was influencing Bambi's behaviour."

"What?" I cried.

"What did you say?" asked Katy.

"I just denied it. I mean, how could I possibly have done it?"

"So what happens now?" asked James.

"Dunno," said Cat, miserably. "I expect more people will come and see Bambi. We can't stop everyone. Someone will like her. I mean, who wouldn't?" She stroked Bambi's ears and Bambi nuzzled her shoulder unhappily.

I couldn't help thinking that Cat was right. Someone would like Bambi, she couldn't keep putting people off. It was only a matter of time before our best-laid plans would fail.

Our misery was interrupted by the arrival of Jessica who'd been filming in the field. She was all smoothed hair, pink trousers and cream shirt and a huge purple gemstone swung from her neck. Opening her car door, she gave us a wave, totally misinterpreting our sombre mood.

"We'll be back tomorrow to take some pictures and film our final scenes and then we'll dismantle everything, get out of your hair and move on to the ice house," she said. "I know we've got in everyone's way," she gestured to the vehicles parked in stupid places, "but tomorrow's pictures will be the most important ones. They'll show the entire foundations of the house which have only just been cleared today. You'll be able to see the pictures in your local museum in the autumn once the programme has been aired. I just want to thank you all for helping us with such an interesting programme and I hope you'll all enjoy watching it."

We all stared at her, glumly.

"Oh, I almost forgot!" she added, turning towards us, her car keys in her hand. "We've added some more fencing around the dig to keep the ponies out – as the foundations have been completely exposed now it's important they're not disturbed. You won't go under the ropes, will you? We've a photographer coming, too, to take the final still pictures for posterity."

"No, don't worry, we won't go anywhere near them," Katy assured her and we all nodded our heads in agreement.

Satisfied, Jessica got in her car and drove off down the drive. We all watched, silently, until the car turned the corner around the laurel bushes and disappeared.

"As if we're interested," sighed James. "Her precious bits of old stone are as safe as houses."

Only that was where James was totally, totally wrong because they weren't. They weren't safe at all. When Bean and I arrived at the yard at the same time the next morning, we were greeted by Katy in a state of high excitement.

"What's up?" I asked, as she galloped towards us.

"You don't want to know!" Katy told me, grimly.

I do, actually, I thought, that's why I asked . . .

"The ponies have all gone through the ropes," she yelled, grabbing Bluey's headcollar and rushing back to the field. "And they've totally trashed the Time Detectives' dig!"

Chapter Twenty-One

"Have you no respect?" I asked Drummer crossly, fastening his headcollar and leading him outside the ropes.

"Something had to be done," he replied, totally unrepentant.

"What, wanton destruction?" I asked him. He'd totally lost the plot this time.

"I can't understand it," said Bean letting Tiffany go outside the ropes and watching her canter off with her nose in the air, her mane and tail flying, "Tiffany's spent the last week going anywhere but the site, snorting and carrying on – and suddenly her life depends on not just going near it, but actually on it. It doesn't make sense."

"It's not like Bluey, either," Katy told us, looking at her blue roan, thoughtfully. "But not because he's like

Tiffany, of course. He's usually so well behaved."

Evicting the other ponies, we mended the ropes and returned to the scene of the crime to put things back the way they were.

"You know what," giggled Bean, "we ought to replace the ropes with POLICE, DO NOT CROSS tape!"

She didn't giggle for very long. Any ideas we'd had of removing the ponies, making good and no-one noticing that anything had happened were squashed as soon as we saw the result of the ponies' night's work.

"I don't know why Time Detectives bothered with a bulldozer," Katy remarked, "when our ponies' digging efforts are nothing short of spectacular."

"Jessica will go spare!" I gulped, remembering her plans for pictures showing the entire foundations of the house. The most important ones, I reminded myself.

The previously orderly site was now in complete disarray. Where there had been neat, rectangular and square lines of foundations there were now deep holes dug up, the dirt thrown around in a terrible mess. Bits of broken stone lay scattered about. Piles of earth littered the site. There was a particularly big hole right in the very centre, like someone was planning a swimming pool. It had gone from organised site to bomb site overnight.

"It looks like a gang of giant moles have been partying," said Katy, grimly, her hands on her hips.

"Who's going to tell Jessica?" I asked.

"Tell her?" asked Bean, her face ashen. "My plan was to scoot off home and let her find out for herself."

"We can't do that!" said Katy.

I agreed. I didn't want to, but I knew we had to explain what had happened. "I'll do it," I said, my heart sinking. "I got her here, after all."

"Phew," sighed Bean. "Well volunteered."

"She's bound to be OK about it," Katy said, smiling at me, "she's so nice."

Yes, I thought, my heart leaping in hope, she is.

"I still don't understand why the ponies did it," Katy mumbled, shaking her head.

"It doesn't really matter now, does it?" I said.

"There's not even any point in trying to make good the mess," Bean said, looking around. "There's just too much work."

"You never know," Katy said, hopefully, "Jessica may even see the funny side!"

There was a short silence as we all contemplated the odds on this happening. They weren't high.

I looked across the field at the guilty party. Drummer stood with Bambi, Moth, Tiffany and Bluey, looking back at us. They didn't look particularly guilty, they looked triumphant. Whatever were they on? And Bluey never did anything naughty – or Moth, for that matter. It just didn't make sense.

Leaving the scene of the crime, we went back to the yard and told James and Dee, who had just arrived, the sorry tale.

"Wasn't my pony!" chimed in Dee, a grim smile on her face. "I'm off the hook with that one, phew!"

"Who's going to tell Jessica?" asked James, just as I had earlier.

"I am," I said, pulling a face.

"I'll come with you, if you like," James volunteered.

My heart leapt. James could be quite the knight in shining armour when he wanted to be. Or perhaps that was just how I liked to interpret it.

"Oh, we'll all come with you," said Katy. "We're all responsible. You didn't think we'd really let you face Jessica alone, did you Pia?"

"I did," mumbled Bean.

"Besides," added Katy, "she's bound to understand how it wasn't our fault."

When Dee told Sophie, her mum just waved her hand in the air dismissively as she led Lester out of his stable and tied him up in the yard.

"Frankly," she said, "I don't really care. The whole Time Detectives thing has been a complete waste of time; they've done nothing to help us, just made things very inconvenient at the yard with all their digging machines, camera crew and whatever. I mean, yesterday, one of the drippy cameramen, the one with the legwear too long to be shorts and too short to be trousers, asked me whether he could have some riding lessons at this riding school of ours. When I told him all the horses and ponies were privately owned he got all huffy and virtually accused me of being a middle-class snob. And that girl with the pigtails goes about half-dressed all the time like she's in some lingerie advert. I'll be glad to see the back of the lot of them. As for that Jessica, if she was any more up herself she'd . . ."

We crept away in full-flow. More doom and gloom wasn't really what we'd been hoping for.

Then Cat and Dec arrived.

"No way!" Cat cried when we told her the news, her jaw dropping. "Shall we saddle up the ponies and make a quick getaway while there's still time?"

This particular plan of action hadn't occurred to me and I thought it had legs.

Brilliant!

Unfortunately, Katy didn't agree and plan A was very much restored.

Poo!

"It's almost ten o'clock," Katy said, looking at her watch. "Jessica will be here any minute now. Oh, here she is!"

I gulped as Jessica's car rumbled down the drive and pulled up by the barn.

"OK," I said, taking a deep breath, "let's do it."

"Hello!" Jessica greeted us with a smile. She was wearing white linen trousers, a blue shirt and lots of silver bangles on both arms which jangled as she walked. The gemstone necklace of the day was big, red and sparkly. "You all look very serious. What's up?"

I focused on her smile. Yeah, Katy was right, she'll be OK about it. A bit miffed, but OK, I told myself.

"Er, well, funny you should ask," I began, a nervous laugh escaping me. How inappropriate, I thought, forcing my face into serious mode. "It's about the site . . ."

"Oh yes, here comes the photographer now," Jessica interrupted me, fixing her hair up on top of her head with a grip. "She's early!"

"I'm afraid she may actually be too late," James butted in.

175

"What do you mean?" asked Jessica, turning to look at James.

"I think you'd better come and take a look," I suggested, walking towards the field. Everyone fell in behind me and we all trooped out to show Jessica the results of the ponies' rampage. As we got nearer, I heard Jessica gasp.

"Wow!" James breathed, surveying the carnage for the first time. "They've done a thorough job, I'll give them that."

"Who did this!" Jessica demanded furiously, her hands on her hips.

I jumped involuntarily and felt my stomach lurch. She so wasn't OK about it.

"The ponies," Katy told her. "They got under the rope."

"They didn't mean it!" said Bean, hopefully.

"Didn't mean it?" cried Jessica. "DIDN'T MEAN IT? How could they not mean it? The site is wrecked. RUINED!"

So she wasn't going to see the funny side either. No surprise, really, considering there wasn't one.

We all stood there, silent. I chewed the inside of my mouth. My face felt hot – I imagined I was probably turning a nice shade of raspberry.

"All that work!" Jessica snapped. "Just one more day – that's all we needed and then your wretched ponies could trash whatever they liked. Just *one* day!"

"It is their field . . ." began Cat, rather rashly, I thought.

Jessica turned on her. Sparks flew out of her eyes and flames gushed from her mouth (or I may have imagined that bit) as she lost it. Completely. I don't remember the exact words because she said it very fast and very, very loud but the gist of it was that we were all very silly little girls who didn't understand the importance of the work she did, and didn't realise that she'd won awards for her docu-dramas, and the last thing she needed was her creativity destroyed by some animals who didn't have the collective brains she had in her little finger, or something like that. Anyway, it wasn't good, that was for sure, and it provoked much flinching from her unwilling audience. Nobody said anything – not even James or Dec at being called silly little girls.

When Jessica stopped screeching I noticed the ponies had all come over to gawk – no doubt amused at the scene they had caused. Then, as Jessica drew breath for another blast, they started heckling.

"Ooooh, get her!" I heard Bambi snigger.

"Talk about overreact!" Drummer added.

"She's not getting it, is she?" Bluey said.

"What a screamer. Tell her to keep it down, can you?" asked Tiffany.

Moth just stood there, her ears going back and forth.

Lining themselves up against the rope they continued to add insult to injury.

As Jessica started her next tirade, ducking under the tape and stamping about in the wreckage of her dig, we were joined by the bemused photographer. The sight of the camera seemed to fill Jessica with further fury – just when we thought it couldn't get any worse.

"There's nothing to photograph!" she screamed. "These, these . . ." she waved her hand towards the ponies, ". . . bloody horses have ruined *everything*."

"Oh," said the photographer, looking grave. She glanced at me and I just shrugged my shoulders and bit my lip.

"Tell that banshee woman to take a proper look," Drummer yelled at me.

I looked at him. Was he for real? Leaving the others, he came over and stood by my side, looking down at the mess below us.

"Tell her," he said, nudging me with his nose.

"Tell her what?" I whispered.

"She's looking in the wrong place," I heard Bambi say.

"That's right – tell her to take a proper look at that big hole we've made," ordered Drummer. "The really *big* one," he added.

I didn't want to. I couldn't see any way any good could come of it and I could imagine Jessica hitting someone if I suggested what Drummer wanted me to suggest. And that someone was likely to be me.

Drummer wasn't going to let it go. He nudged me forward and repeated the order.

"Tell her to look in the big hole. *Tell her!*"

James gave me a funny look. He could tell Drummer was saying something.

I swallowed. Twice. Drummer knew something. This was either the biggest wind-up my pony had ever thought up, or . . .

"Er, Jessica," I began, my voice croaking in fear. "Jessica!"

"WHAT!"

Oh poo.

"I think you need to take a look . . ."

"A GOOD look," Drummer interrupted me.

". . . take a good look in the big hole in the middle."

There. Done. I braced myself. I was soooo dead.

Breathing hard, Jessica narrowed her eyes at me with absolute hatred and made like she was sucking a lemon. She didn't move. She didn't look in the big hole.

"I'll look," said James, ducking under the rope, jumping into the hole and peering downwards.

Nobody said anything. At least Jessica had shut up yelling.

"Found it yet?" asked Bambi. All the ponies leaned against the rope and gazed down intently at James. And so did everyone else. I had a sudden vision of buried treasure, a pirate's chest overflowing with gold coins and treasures. Oh, if only . . .

"Well?" Jessica asked, folding her arms and looking militant.

"Er, well, I can't see anything, just a few bits of broken tiles . . . It looks like someone's old bathroom in here," James said, squatting down and poking the soil with his hands.

"WHAT?" yelled Jessica, leaping over the mounds of earth to kneel down beside James with a sudden and urgent interest.

"Oh my God!!!" she exclaimed, scrabbling away at the dirt with her bare hands as though her life depended on it. "Oh my . . . !"

"At last!" Drummer said, tutting. "I thought she'd never get there."

"Come on," said Bambi, turning to go, "our work here is done."

"Oi!" I said, grabbing Drummer's mane behind his ears and anchoring him to the spot. "Don't just hit-and-run like that. What's going on?"

"Ouch, let go!" Drummer ordered me, shaking his head.

"Not likely!" I told him. "Spill the beans!"

"She's found what she's been looking for," Bluey told me. "Only she didn't know it was here so she wasn't actually looking for it, so we had to help a bit."

"It's been right under her nose all the time," said Drum, "only she's been concentrating on all that recent stuff. If she had our senses, she'd have known it was there all along."

"We thought you'd find it by yourselves," Bambi butted in, "but no. Honestly, it's a wonder you lot can do anything without us."

"Now give over with the headlock, will you?" Drum asked.

"What's going on, Pia?" Releasing Drummer I turned around to see Cat, Bean, Katy and Dec all looking at me quizzically.

"I'm not sure," I told them, looking down at Jessica scrabbling away in the mud, her white linen trousers caked in dirt. "But it seems the ponies did this deliberately to unearth something the Time Detectives crew missed."

"I don't believe it, I don't believe it!" Jessica yelled, hugging James (*Oi, you can cut that out*, I thought).

"What is it?" asked Katy.

"It's priceless, just priceless!" Jessica told us, her eyes shining. "I'll have to get the team in of course but by the look of it there's an original Roman mosaic under here."

"And that's . . . good?" asked Bean.

"Good? GOOD? It's better than good!" Jessica yelled. "If it is what I think it is," she continued, "Mr Collins can kiss goodbye to building any houses on this site!"

Chapter Twenty-Two

Nobody heard what Robert Collins had to say about his priceless Roman mosaic, but it turned out that it wasn't actually his. National Heritage changed their tune in an instant and suddenly decided that the site belonged to the nation. End of. Bit fickle of them, we all thought, still miffed at their initial attitude when they hadn't wanted to know, but as they were hobbling Robert Collins's development plans, we decided to forgive them.

"So now what will happen to Laurel Farm?" Katy had asked, when Jessica told us that filming would continue and once they had enough for their revised programme, National Heritage would take over and protect the site.

"They'll probably want to remove the mosaic and take it somewhere else to clean it up and display it where it can't be damaged by the elements. They'll definitely want to see what other Roman remains lie around here, I mean, the Romans didn't just build mosaics in the middle of nowhere. There was probably a villa here," Jessica had told us, back to her usual smiley self. She was also back in her pristine clothes – some light blue trousers and a tight navy sweater under a cream jacket. An azure blue gemstone swung from a chain around her neck and a large gold ring swamped her hand. Her dark hair was tied back with a scarf. Since her lapse after the ponies' bouncing about on the site, she was back in control and looking her usual, smooth self.

"So does that mean . . . ?" I asked, gulping.

"Yes, Pia, Robert Collins will *not* be building on that land," laughed Jessica. "It will take National Heritage an age to uncover the mosaic properly, and until they've examined the whole site, any building work is on hold. Permanently! They'll probably want the ponies moved, though," she added. "After all, they're not exactly careful where they put their hooves, are they?"

That's where you're wrong, I thought. The ponies knew exactly where to put their hooves. She didn't think finding the mosaic was accidental, did she?

"Who knows what 2000-year-old Roman treasures are yet to be discovered," Jessica said, smiling in excitement.

I bet there's more than a villa, I thought to myself, remembering that I found Epona a mile or so away. I wouldn't be surprised if there'd been a whole cavalry barracks and a fort somewhere nearby, too.

"But that's the ponies' field," said Bean. "Where will they go?"

"I shouldn't worry too much," Jessica assured us. "Robert Collins will receive compensation for the land – and we've looked into it, the farmer is perfectly willing to sell the field next door so the ponies can go there. You'll just have the gate in a different place – and, of course, the ponies won't have such a great view, but I don't suppose they'll mind!"

"But what's to stop Robert Collins building on *that* field?" asked Katy.

"Oh, that won't happen!" snapped Jessica. "Once this field's had a thorough going-over, National Heritage will probably move on to that one, letting you have the old field back. There's no telling how big a Roman site might be."

"That's fantastic!" yelled Bean, breaking into a smile.

"And don't think we've forgotten the ice house!"

Jessica said, beaming at us.

I had. Totally. Once I'd realised it couldn't save Robert Collins building Laurel Heights, I had banished it from my thoughts.

"The Time Detectives are, even as I speak, taking a look at things over there now and examining it inside. Alex is over there with them," added Jessica.

"What could they possibly find over there?" poo-pooed Dee. "It's just full of nothing."

"Interesting, though," Jessica said, "it's an ingenious construction. It will make a fascinating footnote to our programme. The public loves that sort of thing. Anything dark and spooky goes down very well."

We all stared at the mess that used to be our ponies' field. Much more securely fenced now (even though Drummer had assured me they wouldn't go near it now they'd found what they'd been looking for), the Time Detectives had erected a tent over the precious mosaic to protect it from the weather, and it was surrounded by even more hills of mud and old stones dug up by equine hooves and human machines. The field looked more like a bomb site than pasture.

"Let's go and look at the other field," suggested Katy, and we all trooped from the gate to the other side of the school to see the field in question. It was bigger

than the existing field, with four big trees dotted abou
a border of hedging and some gentle slopes.

"It's actually really nice," said Bean.

"The ponies will love it," I said.

"We've really done it!" said James. "We've really saved the stables. Stables SOS has actually worked."

"I can't believe it, not after all this time," murmured Cat.

"Thanks to the ponies," I said. I was going to give Drummer the best meal ever tonight, I decided, with carrots and apples and sugar beet. He so deserved it – and so did the others.

"If only Mrs Collins wasn't going into a home," said Katy.

"Oh, yes, poor Mrs Collins," said Bean.

"What's all that noise?" I said, turning back to the yard. There was a right commotion going on and we all walked back to find out what it was. One of the Time Detectives, the girl with the pigtails who never wore much, was talking to Jessica. I say talking, she was panting, her breath coming out in distressed gasps, and she looked as white as a sheet. We all went closer, shamelessly wanting to find out what had stressed her out so much.

"Start from the beginning, Chelsea," Jessica told her,

holding her arms. They were shaking, I noticed.

"Horatio found it!" the girl said, shuddering.

"Found what?" asked Jessica, gently.

Horatio? I thought. There's a cool name. It could only be the Time Detective with the plaited beard. He was so an Horatio.

"It was right at the very bottom, under some branches someone had thrown in. Horatio had already gone all the way down with Alex and they were lifting up the branches and looking underneath. Horatio was swinging his torch when it shone right on it . . ." she gulped again and shuddered, her hand over her mouth as though she couldn't bear to talk about it.

"Oh, come on," James muttered impatiently, "get a grip!"

"On what?" Jessica asked.

"It was lying there – all white and . . . and . . . oh, it was horrible, just like in the films, only it was really there," said Chelsea, her face in her hands.

"I'm bored now," I heard James whisper to me. I stifled a giggle. What Chelsea said next made it no laughing matter – and it cured James's boredom, for sure.

"We found a body!" Chelsea said, dramatically. "There's a skeleton at the bottom of the ice house!"

Chapter Twenty-Three

James, Cat and Dee were all for saddling up and galloping up to the ice house for a look-see. Katy, Bean and I were definitely in the other camp – the one which considered that to be a very bad idea.

My thoughts immediately flew back to what Jazz, the traveller girl had said when she'd first gone into the ice house. It has the feel of a *grob*, she had said. And *grob*, she'd explained to me, meant *tomb*. She was bang on! And, remembering other things that my pony had said, I was going to tackle Drummer as well. He'd kept it from me – he'd known all along. What else did he know about the surrounding area that he wasn't telling?

Of course, in the end nobody could go to the ice house because Jessica called the police and the whole area *was* marked off with POLICE DO NOT CROSS tape. Which was spooky considering that had been Bean's idea when the ponies had trashed the dig site.

The whole yard could talk of nothing else. Who was the mysterious skeleton? How long had they been down there? Was it an accident – someone falling in and breaking something so they couldn't climb out – or did it indicate something far more sinister?

"If it's recent, I think I'm going to do a Tiffany," said Bean, shuddering.

"What do you mean?" Cat asked her.

"FREAK OUT!" yelled Bean, losing it already.

"Oh, it's probably years and years old, Bean," said James.

"I bet it's Adam Rowe," said Dee, her eyes like saucers. "Slowly suffocating in an underground tomb is a pretty bad death."

"You don't know he suffocated," said Katy.

"Or do you?" asked James, holding the front of his polo shirt like it had lapels and addressing us in a pompous voice in the manner of a crown prosecutor. He turned to Dee. "It seems to me, Miss Wiseman, that you know more than you should!"

"Who's Adam Rowe?" asked Cat.

Oh no, I thought, not again.

The next day Jessica told us that the police had

found another body. There were two bodies in the ice house.

"The police are treating it as suspicious," she said, to her enthralled audience – us.

"You don't say!" Drummer said across the yard in his best sarcastic voice.

"What do you know about it?" I yelled back. Jessica looked at me like I was a stirrup short of a saddle.

"I'm saying nothing," replied Drummer, innocence personified. I hate it when he does that.

"Are you going to find a body a day?" asked James, grinning.

"If only, James," Jessica replied. "Our ratings would go sky high!"

News of the police findings trickled back to us over the next few days. The bodies were old, from early last century. They were a man and a woman. And then, the news that gave us all the heebie-jeebies, they had been murdered.

"How do they know?" Bean asked Jessica, once she had managed to disentangle her from digging around the Roman mosaic. The field was full of people – some from National Heritage – all clambering over and around it, determined to examine every centimetre. It had become impossible to turn the ponies out and the new field next door had been hastily commandeered, much to the ponies' delight – it had much more grass so they were all out gorging and making like they were deaf whenever we called them to go riding.

"There are all sorts of tests they can do, Bean," Jessica answered her, "and the fact that the male skeleton has a huge hole in the back of his skull is a big clue. The woman, apparently, had her neck broken."

"Ugh, how horrid!" Bean said, pulling a face.

"The big news," Jessica continued, "is that they found a valuable gold ring still on the man's finger and this is the lead they've been looking for. They can identify him from it."

"Why didn't whoever murdered him take the ring?" James asked.

"It's a very distinctive ring," Jessica told us solemnly. "I doubt the murderer would have been able to sell it without being traced."

We had to wait several days before we got the next exciting instalment, not from Jessica but from Alex Willard. He had been so enthralled by developments that he had stayed on longer than he'd planned and told us the new piece of the puzzle. Did I say exciting? I meant MIND BLOWING!!!

"It's now certain that the skeletons are one of the

Rowe family and a local girl called Agatha Turnball who used to work at the big house," he told us. "Are you all right, Bean?"

Bean had turned white. She tended to do that whenever the name Rowe was mentioned, and I'm sure I paled, too. James, however, together with Dee, grabbed the news with ghoulish glee.

"Another member of the Rowe family!" Dee said, her eyes shining. "For just how long did the house belong to the Rowes?"

"Oh, hundreds of years," Alex told her.

"It sounds like they all had a colourful time of it," said James, "getting themselves murdered all over the place."

"I wonder why *that* Rowe was murdered," said Dee.

"And the girl, don't forget she was a victim, too," Katy reminded us all.

"Everyone had thought they'd run off together, and that was why the son never inherited," Alex continued.

"You mean the one in the ice house is the eldest son?" I asked, realising the significance of it. He'd disappeared, but he hadn't got as far as everyone had thought. I shuddered. Everyone had believed the eldest son had eloped with his lady love from the village, but in fact the two of them had got no further than a dark and dismal tomb in the depths of the woods.

"That's so sad!" cried Katy, her hand flying to her mouth. "And I thought it was so romantic, the two of them running off, not worried about the fortune he was leaving behind, unable to face the scandal of him marrying beneath him, yet even less able to live without each other. But all the time they've been in the ice house, dead."

"Who killed them?" asked James.

"The younger son of course!" yelled Dee.

"Well, nobody actually knows for sure," Alex said, "but it seems fairly likely."

"After all," Dee butted in, "he did the old man in, too!"

"That was my idea!" said James, a bit miffed.

"Oh, who cares who thought of it?" said Dee. "I bet that's what happened, don't you?"

"Absolutely!" said Katy. "The youngest son did in both his brother and Adam, his father. What a nasty piece of work!"

"I think you're probably right," said Alex, "but why do you think the father was called Adam?"

Poo. Explain that one, I thought.

"Wasn't he?" Katy asked, innocently.

"No," said Alex, frowning. "The father was called

Ralph and the youngest brother was Luke."

I felt a huge wave of relief. That séance was pure nonsense after all.

"It was the eldest son," said Alex, "the one we found in the ice house with a hole in his skull where someone had hit him with a sharp instrument. His name was Adam."

Everyone gasped and fell silent. Except Alex. He had no idea how that small sentence could have such an effect on his audience.

"Well if *that's* not a 'bad death'," said Dee, shakily, breaking the silence at last, "then I don't know what is."

Chapter Twenty-Four

"Oh, look out, here comes know-all," murmured Drummer, shaking his head and making his tie-up ring on the wall rattle. I stopped picking out his off fore and looked up to see who he was talking about. I didn't know Drummer called him that, I thought. How rude!

"I've come to say good bye," Alex said, giving me a hug. "Take care of yourself, Pony Whisperer Pia."

"Oh," I said, "must you go?"

"I'm afraid so," Alex replied, grinning. "I have work to do, you know. This little escapade has been very interesting but I have equine clients at home that need some therapy. And when you gotta go, you gotta go!"

I supposed my plan for Alex and my mum would never have worked out really, I thought with a sinking heart. And besides, if it had, we would probably have moved to Alex's place and, much as I loved the thought of living such an equine fairy tale, deep down I didn't want to leave Laurel Farm. Drummer certainly didn't. Now we'd saved the stables I didn't want us to go anywhere. What had I been thinking of?

The trouble with you, Pia, I told myself, is that you don't think things through. Stop and go through the consequences of any plans next time.

"Oh, and Jessica asked me to give you this," said Alex, handing me an envelope. He winked as he said it, which I thought was odd. "It's for all of you, all of you who helped Jessica find the mosaic."

"What do you mean?" asked Drummer, indignantly. "She didn't find it, we did – Moth, Bluey, Tiffany, Bambi and I. Jessica found diddly-squat."

"Shhhh!" I told him, thinking how ungrateful the ponies would be about a thank-you card, which was obviously what the envelope contained. They'd rather have a sack of carrots, I thought.

"What's Drum saying?" asked Alex.

"He's just sorry to see you go," I lied, stuffing the envelope in my pocket with Epona.

"Coward!" snorted Drummer.

"If you ever need any help with any more adventures, you know where to reach me," Alex said, smiling. "And say goodbye to your mother for me, won't you. She's a wonderful woman and that chap Mike is a lucky man. I wouldn't be surprised if you're asked to be a bridesmaid before too long."

I froze. Did he really mean what I thought he meant? My mum? Mike-the-bike? The shock subsided. Actually, I thought, I wouldn't mind that at all. Mum seemed really chilled nowadays and Mike was easy to get on with. Not like some of my mother's ex-boyfriends. I shrugged my shoulders. As long as I didn't have to wear some pig-awful peach number and have my hair styled. I was far too old to want to be a bridesmaid, for goodness sake.

"Aren't you going to see Carol again?" I asked him, my eyes wide and innocent. Alex gave me a look.

"She really liked you," I said, rubbing it in. Alex, ever polite, smiled.

"And I liked her," he lied. "Now don't forget you're welcome to visit any time you and your family are in my neck of the woods. I mean it Pia, any time!"

I grinned and nodded and we had a bit of a hug and then Alex got in his car and drove off down the drive, with me waving after him like mad.

Alex Willard is my *friend*, I thought to myself.

It sounded so weird.

My mobile went. My heart sank as I flipped it open.

"Pia!" a voice shouted out from it.

"Hi, Dad!" I replied, hearing Drummer sigh beside me.

"Just thought I'd let you know that Lyn and I have found the most lovely cottage with a couple of acres in Bickacre. We're putting in an offer and the great news is that when you come and stay with us, you'll be able to bring Drummer with you!"

Was that good, I thought? Bickacre was a couple of villages away. What did they want a couple of acres for?

"Lyn's decided she really wants to live in the country," Dad went on, "she's going to get a goat."

She gets my goat, I thought, imagining a goat pulling Skinny along, nibbling her washing on the line, getting into her country kitchen. She'd obviously been watching too many of those "moving to the country" programmes on the telly. That wouldn't last, I thought. I'd give it one winter, tops.

"That's fabulous, Dad," I said, ringing off after promising I'd go and stay with them soon and wondering how I could get out of it. I finished grooming Drummer and went for a ride with Bean – carefully avoiding going anywhere near the ice house.

"This is blissful," Bean said, closing her eyes and tilting her face up to catch the warmth of the sun.

"We've saved the stables after all – whaaaa!"

Tiffany stopped dead and snorted at a plastic carrier bag hanging off a branch. Pushing herself back off Tiffany's neck, Bean recovered her composure.

"What a stupid place to hang washing," muttered Tiffany.

"Of course," Drummer said, "the other, more pressing problem is still with us."

I said nothing. When it came to Bambi, we had failed. There was no good way to say it.

It wasn't until we got back to the yard and I dismounted in the yard that I remembered the thank-you note. Pulling it out of my pocket, I got everyone's attention.

"Alex gave me this," I said, waving the envelope in the air. "It's to all of us."

"What is it?" asked James, yawning.

"I'll read it," I replied, ripping open the envelope. There it was, the suspected thank-you note. It wasn't quite how I had imagined it, though.

'*Dear Pia, Katy, Bean, Cat, Dee and James,*' I read out, '*Here is a share of the proceeds from the sale of the ring found on Adam Rowe in the ice house, to the local museum. Over 400 years old, the ring belonged to one of the original Rowes. It was decided by the powers that be that it should belong to the nation as there are no more Rowes living now, so I want you to have a share of its value to enjoy. I know you will spend it wisely. It was great working with you all – without you I would never have found the Roman mosaic!'*

"Is she still taking the credit for that?" exclaimed Drummer, miffed.

'*I hope you'll enjoy watching the programme when it is aired. Thanks again, love Jessica.*'

"Oh wow!" exclaimed Dee, "a reward!"

"How much is it, Pia?" asked Katy.

"Pah, fifty quid tops!" snorted James.

I unfolded the cheque inside the card. It was made out to Sophie but with a note stapled to it to say it was to be shared between us all.

"Oh!" I gasped.

Five heads all crammed over my shoulders.

"Is that three noughts?" asked Katy, incredulously.

I nodded, my mouth open in shock. I held in my hand a cheque for two thousand pounds.

Chapter Twenty-Five

"Where is everyone?" I asked Katy, propping my bike up against the wall.

"Dee's at a show, the others are riding," Katy replied. "Me and Bluey are entered for a working hunter class at Pinewood show tomorrow, which is why I'm giving him a bath. Are you going?"

"I am actually," I told her, going to give Bluey a pat on the neck, but changing my mind and stroking his nose instead, because that was a dry bit. "I've entered Drummer for the riding club pony class and I thought we'd have a stab at the tack and turnout – and the clear round, of course. I'll get Drummer in and give him a bath, too."

"It's such a lovely hot day," Katy said, sticking her thumb on the end of the hose so that it sprayed over Bluey's legs. Bluey lifted up first one hind leg then the other in response to its icyness. I knew Drummer would go on and on about the temperature of the water, even though it was a hot day. I wondered whether I might lock Epona in my tackbox so I wouldn't have to listen to him going on about it.

The bay pony in question was waiting by the gate looking fed up when I went to get him in from the field. The *new* field. It meant only Pippin and Henry would be left out there tearing at the grass.

No Bambi there, of course.

When Drummer saw Bluey surrounded by water he threw up his head and rolled his eyes.

"Pur-leese tell me I'm not in for all that nonsense!" he said dramatically.

"Oh, don't make such a fuss," I told him, tying him up outside his stable. A pale rectangle with two empty screw holes showed where Bambi's nameplate used to hang on the stable next door.

"You want to look nice for the show tomorrow, don't you?" I asked Drummer.

"A show? First I've heard about it!"

Ignoring the histrionics, I was just working a lather up on Drummer's mane when I heard a muffled banging noise. We all heard it. Drummer and Bluey turned to look whilst Katy and I stared at each other in alarm.

It was coming from Mrs Collins's house.

"What was that?" I asked.

Katy shrugged her shoulders.

"There it is again!" I said, as the banging continued and then stopped.

"It sounds to me," began Drummer, "that Mrs C's house is no longer empty."

"Do you think Robert Collins is in there?" I asked Katy.

She shook her head. "His car's not here – it can't be him."

"You don't think...?" I said, walking across the yard to whisper to her.

"What?"

"You don't think it could be Mrs Collins, do you?"

"You mean...?"

"Popped her clogs and come back to haunt us?"

Katy lifted her head in that sensible way she does. "No!" she said, decisively. "But I think we ought to investigate, even so."

I didn't like the sound of that but before I could protest, Katy walked up to the door of the house and knocked purposefully on it. I crept up behind her, not wanting to appear nervous, even though I was. That whole body-in-the-ice house thing (sorry, bod-ies, plural) had got to me.

Without warning the door was wrenched open and both Katy and I took a step back when we saw who it was standing in front of us in her dressing gown and slippers, Twiddles cradled in her arms and Squish by her side.

She looked real enough.

"Mrs Collins, is that really you?" I asked, hardly daring to breathe.

"Of course it is," she replied, crossly. "Who else would it be?"

"It's just that, well, we thought . . ." began Katy. She stopped, unsure how to go on.

"You thought what?"

"Er, well we thought your son was going to take over running this place," Katy said, surprised into telling the truth.

"Humph!" snorted Mrs Collins, throwing back her head. For one terrible moment I thought she was going to spit. Tiddles narrowed his eyes at us – but because he was in Mrs Collins's arms he couldn't very well do his evil cat act, he had to maintain his cuddly puss persona. I could see how much it was hurting him. I felt no sympathy.

"My son," began Mrs C, drawing herself up to her

full height of at least five feet nothing in her slippered feet, "had some fancy ideas about this place, which he isn't smart enough to keep to himself!" she snapped. "I leave the place for a minute and when I come back the field's all dug up like there's a motorway going through it, some TV people are telling me what I can and can't do on my own land, the National Heritage busy-bodies are yakking on about me swapping my perfectly good field for another one and the only good thing to come out of it is some talk of compensation, which I don't mind admitting, I have a use for. And I've lost a livery which I can ill afford – if I'd been in hospital any longer I dare say I'd have come back to a yard of empty boxes and no rent coming in. Honestly, I can't turn my back on this place for a second without it all going to pot."

"But your son . . ." began Katy.

"Enough!" snapped Mrs C, holding up her hand. "I know all about his scheme and it's never going to happen. The only way he's ever going to get his greedy little hands on this place is when I'm carried out feet first, and that's not going to be for a long, long time, especially now I've got my pacemaker!" She tapped at her chest and glared at us, her grey hair framing her face like some ghastly silver halo.

I glanced at Katy, and she looked back at me. This was music to our ears.

"Now I've got to go," continued Mrs C, turning around and shuffling back into the hall. "I've got those stair lift people coming to measure up and take some of that compensation money off my hands. Make sure the yard is tidy and don't leave the hose running – there was a huge puddle when I came back last night. I hope that Charlotte girl isn't washing her hair up here again! I've told her about that."

"No, Mrs C!" we said in unison as the front door was shut in our faces.

"Wow!" breathed Katy. "I don't think we ought to get her wound up like that again, she might have another heart attack, pacemaker or no pacemaker."

"I don't know why we ever doubted that she would return," I said. "She's as tough as old boots."

"I bet son Robert got a right old telling off!" giggled Katy.

"Phew, I wouldn't like to have been in his shoes when his mum found out about his scheme," I said, remembering how I'd imagined Robert Collins intimidating his mother. How wrong was I?

"You do realise, don't you," said Katy, "that there was never any chance of Robert Collins building on the ponies' field. All that planning, all that disruption, all that . . . that . . . *angst* was for nothing!"

"Well," I said, giving her a look, "not quite *nothing*."

Everything was back to normal.

Almost.

Chapter Twenty-Six

I looked across the yard in the evening light to gaze at Drummer, my eyes glancing to the adjoining stable where a new, brass nameplate successfully covered the mark left by the old one.

Hearing footsteps, I turned around.

"Hey there, Pony Whisperer!" said James, grinning at me.

I grinned back. "I didn't know you were still here."

"I've just been around the new field again," he explained, holding up a couple of lengths of baler twine. "I found these – the farmer used to make hay on that field, and every time I walk around it, I find some more old string."

"I'll help you find some more tomorrow, if you like," I told him. I wouldn't mind that, I thought, a chance to spend some time alone with James.

"Am I *ever* going out tonight?" called Drummer.

"OK," I told him, walking over and leading him out on to the yard.

"I'll come with you," offered James, and the three of us walked past the outdoor school and to the field. James stayed by the gate as I led Drummer inside and took off his headcollar, offering him a carrot.

"Thanks," he mumbled. Then he stopped chewing and looked into my eyes, nuzzling my elbow gently. "And thanks for, well, *you* know," he added.

Smiling, I stroked his nose. It was like velvet.

"You're welcome, Drummer. You know there's nothing I wouldn't do for you," I whispered to him, thinking back to the day I'd thrown my Hickstead sash into the flames. It had been worth it after all, I thought. Drummer was my most favourite person in the whole world.

"Yeah, well, likewise," my pony replied, "and that's why I've had a word," he added, walking off to meet up with the object of his desire, asking her whether she'd enjoyed her ride out with Tiffany and Moth earlier.

"What do you mean?" I called after him, puzzled, but he didn't explain.

It had taken about three minutes for everyone to agree what we would all buy with the reward cheque.

It had been a unanimous, total no-brainer, and I only fleetingly allowed myself to imagine spending three-hundred-and-thirty-three pounds (the six-way split which Dee calculated immediately on account of her posh education – we were all counting on our fingers when she put us out of our misery with a derisive snort) on some new tack for Drummer. I knew he would be all for the final, collective decision.

"It's great to see them together, they really do adore each other, don't they?" said James, leaning his elbows on the gate and watching Drummer and Bambi nibble each other's withers.

I nodded. Our combined reward monies had bought us a skewbald mare for the person who loved her most – apart from Drummer. It had been a good buy, without strings.

"She's totally yours," our elected spokesperson Katy had told an overwhelmed Cat. "We all want you to have Bambi. It will be exactly the same as before – you always paid for her keep. Well now she's yours *completely*."

"Are you sure?" Cat had said, shaking her head in disbelief. Then she had wept a lot and hugged everyone – even me – and couldn't stop thanking us, and I think everyone had been a bit emotional. Even James had looked choked up but had managed to turn it into a cough. Looking at Drummer and Bambi together now, I knew we had spent the money wisely. Aunt Pam had taken nothing but Bambi's nameplate to put on her stable at the bottom of her garden – apparently Emily had set her heart on having a Bambi pony, so now she had a stable and a nameplate – perfect pony to come.

James and I watched Drummer and Bambi wander off into the sunset together. How perfect it all was. I sighed. I could just hear them talking as they walked away from us. I was wrong, things weren't so perfect.

"You're looking a bit round these days, aren't you?" I heard Drummer say, looking Bambi over.

"What are you saying?" Bambi replied, huffily, her head rising in indignation.

"Only that I hope you're not letting yourself go," Drummer said.

"Letting myself GO?" Bambi cried, flattening her ears on to her neck and snaking her head at Drummer in fury.

"Keep your mane on!" said Drum, "I only said . . ."

It was exactly like when my mum had got fed up with her new boyfriends. At least that wasn't happening with Mike-the-bike. Quite the opposite. Don't tell me the novelty was wearing off between Drummer and

Bambi after we'd gone to so much trouble!

"What are they saying?" asked James, tilting his head as he turned to look at me, his hair flopping over one ear.

"Oh, nothing," I lied, my stomach doing a flip.

"Do you know, Pia," James went on, "even if we hadn't all got that cheque from Jessica I know we would have saved Bambi for Cat somehow. You were so determined to do it."

Uh-oh, I thought. I'm getting credit I don't deserve again. A change of subject was needed. "Does anyone know where Leanne has moved Mr Higgins to?" I asked.

"That snotty Box Meadow Stables where she can concentrate on her dressage," James replied. "Anyway, who cares? She never really made an effort to fit in. I won't miss her."

"I wonder who we'll get in Mr Higgins's old stable?" I said, matching James's posture as I leaned on the gate and watched the ponies in their new field. I hoped it would be someone nice, and a horse or pony that would get on with the others. And it occurred to me that whoever it was, *they* would be the newbie – not me. At last!

"Did you know that Bean's going out with Declan

tomorrow night?" James asked ever so casually, picking at a splinter on the gate.

"Oh. No, I didn't," I said, deciding I'd call Bean later and give her a hard time. She'd kept that quiet!

"They're going to see a film," James explained, still working intently at the splinter.

Why hadn't Bean said anything, I wondered? I'd have thought, after all we'd been through . . .

"So, er, Drummer suggested you might like to go, too," said James.

"Drummer did?" I asked, puzzled. James was supposed to talk to Moth when he borrowed Epona, not Drummer, I thought. "Well, Drummer's got that wrong," I said, frowning. "I'd be a right gooseberry."

"No you wouldn't," James replied, giving me a look, "not if you were with me."

My heart started thumping. Surely James could hear it? Surely the whole world could hear it? How stupid was I? What else had Drummer had a word about, I thought, hardly daring to go there. Just how much did James know about my feelings for him? I had a sudden urge to run across the field and tackle my pony.

"Er, yeah, OK, that would be great," I said instead, not daring to look at James. There was just one thing . . .

"Er, James, I just want you to know . . ." I began, the karma thing thudding away in my brain – you know – getting back what you dish out and everything.

"Yeah?"

"Um, I just wanted you to know that the reason I wanted to save Bambi for Cat was really for Drummer's sake. I didn't do it for Cat – like you seem to think."

"Oh. I see. Well, in that case, the date's off," said James, looking at me sternly.

My heart skipped a beat. Karma my . . .

"Not really!" laughed James. "I know you love that bay pony more than anything in the world. I can recognise competition when I see it!"

And that bay pony, I realised with a grin, loved me back!

"We've saved Bambi, we've saved the stables," I sighed, feeling like I was going to burst, "and Cat and I are almost chummy. Do you think we could all go back to doing some normal things now? Riding and going to shows and having some fun?"

"Normal!" snorted James. "What's *normal* to the Pony Whisperer?"

I laughed. James was right. Normal was never going to be an option with Epona in my pocket and the ponies turning everyday happenings inside out, back-to-front and upside down.

And *that*, I decided, was just how I liked it!